BORDERLINE

ROYAL POFF

Edited and formatted by 360 Editing (a division of Uncomfortably Dark).

Editor: Candace Nola

Paperback Cover Art by Don Noble.

Hardcover Cover Art by Leonard Sihoming and Fabled Beast Design (A.A. Medina).

their lives."-Megan Stockton, author of Bluejay and Dark & Deep

"Royal Poff created a beautifully horrific cosmic horror that will both terrify you and break your heart. Touching on the realities of what it's like to deal with mental illness and addiction, this novella is visceral, filled to the brim with gore and an utterly petrifying cosmic being."-River Gardner, author of Good-Bye, Valentine

Contents

Dedication

I dedicate this book to my mom, Kristy Poff, first and foremost, for shaping me into the person I am today. To my Aunt Joy, and Pap, William Poff, for always urging me forward when pursuing my dreams. To my Mama J, Jamie Blackhart, and my father Joe Ortlieb, for never giving up on me. To my Nana, Phyllis Houska, for being my personal therapist during emotional times.

To all my siblings, DJ, Mena, Dharma, Raven, Finnley, and Autumn, for being my pillars of happiness in an unforgiving world. To all my amazing friends, Faye Corbin, Logan Masenheimer, Emma Sites, and many more.

And to anyone who finds themselves in need of the kinship of another broken, messy soul. I see you. I feel you. You are loved.

PROLOGUE

PAST

TWO POLICEMEN FOUGHT THEIR way through a sea of black as they approached a quaint, ramshackle house that grew from the ground like a wilted flower. The men were briefly backlit by a revolving pair of blue and red lights, flashing with a robotic consistency. The first, and the taller of the two, itched his pistol's holster as he stepped tentatively up to the door which sat ajar, dangling on its hinge and quivering in the cool November wind. He bore beady eyes that squinted as they took in the faint traces of blood on the doorway. Even before entering the house, the smell of rot met them at the door, slapping their senses into a caustic overdrive, as if they couldn't help but take in the smell on some primal urge, almost hungry for more.

"What the fuck?" his partner whispered. He was a portlier man with a far less experienced stance. He heralded a stereotypical cop mustache that sat atop pursed lips, souring at the intense aroma. He tugged on the neck of his spotless uniform, prying it from the skin that rolled over it slightly.

The first figure bent down, running a finger along the blood and holding it up to the light as it switched hues once more. Quietly, he unholstered his firearm, placing one hand on its grip as he entered the house. The inside was an all-consuming darkness, so all there was to guide him was the slight flurry of light that permeated through the windows. He strode inside, guided by the tugging curiosity in his gut as his partner followed close behind. They walked in, edging the wall, and feeling around for a light switch of any kind. The paneling was cold, as if the heat had been off for a while.

He stumbled a few more steps before his hand landed on the light switch, flicking it to life, and immediately wished he hadn't. Three bodies were slung about the room in various positions, cast aside like rag dolls with their limbs bent at impossible angles. The first figure had a twisted, mangled form as their body lay stretched out like one of those movie chalk outlines, cloaked in a trail of blood showcasing they had crawled at least two yards across the floor before succumbing to their wounds. Another lay sprawled across the table, multiple kitchen knives stabbed into their back like a pincushion, erupting from their spine in no discernable pattern. The last body lay on the couch, the throat slit clean through.

"I thought this call was for a fucking OD," the portly man said, but the other merely shushed him.

He held up a finger to wait, and both figures held their breath so they could listen to their surroundings. A round of barely audible knocking issued from the adjacent room. Both figures silently glided through the darkness, allowing their Glocks to lead them as they turned the corner into the other room.

Empty. Entirely, hauntingly empty. The aged furniture coated in a collection of filth coated tchotchkes, marking that the house had been sitting abandoned for quite some time. An old-style box TV sat in the middle of the room; its sides spray painted, and the glass smashed in. A moth-eaten couch sat next to it, equally coated in graffiti. The knocking continued, increasing in intensity as they traversed the room, crunching broken glass beneath their feet. They twitched at each pop, sending shivers down their spines as the taller officer followed a bleeding river trail that was freshly stained into the carpet.

They turned a corner where a kid stood in the exact center of the room, swaying, his body covered in blood as his foot tapped the ground over and over. His hands gripped his skull so tight he nearly pulled out his hair. He held a glittering silver blade in his one hand, coated in blood that danced far too close to his eye.

"Shut up, shut up, shut up," he chanted, over and over. He was a teenager, around the same age as the bodies, barely pushing his way past adolescence.

"Kid, put down the knife," the taller of the cops commanded in a stern but compassionate tone.

"It's in my skin," he wailed, ignoring the cop completely. "It's in my skin and it won't get out. I can hear it behind my eyes." His head whipped in their direction, crazed eyes bouncing around as if taking in a million details at once. "They're inside of me!" he squealed.

"Drop the knife, son." The cop's hand shook as adrenaline flooded his veins. He wasn't used to this kind of thing happening, not in a small town like this.

The boy lunged at them, knife poised, and was shot immediately, his body spring-boarding backward. As he clattered to the ground, a small pill bottle rolled free from his hand.

1

—.—

FEAR OF ABANDONMENT

PRESENT

A SINGLE FIGURE STALKED his looming shadow as he straddled the spotlight irises that cascaded from the wallowing streetlights, feet exploding into fireworks of droplets as they kicked up puddles. They trudged on, head buckled to fog any features and hair matted down by the rain. A single car croaked past, trapping the details of the stranger for a brief second in the headlights before returning to the realm of shadows.

He was lanky, with spindly legs that buckled slightly with each robotic turnover. His chest was concave, jutting out a mountain range of boney back muscles that heaved as he breathed, eyes continuously transfixed on the splashing tremors his feet caused. His eyes traced a passing car, head barely raising. His muscles tensed for a second, as if fighting the urge to jump after the car until it raced from view. The night howled, pushing through the man's hair as he huddled against the cold. He lapped the campus eight times, each step monotonously restricted to the same padded tempo as the last, a fiddle-footed parade that only stopped every time he crossed paths with a single entrance that taunted him. The entrance appeared more like a lair than the college dorm he knew it was.

His path crossed with another voyager at the intersection of a lamp, his frame expelling the light that her legs consumed. He perused her feet, not bothering to raise his head any higher. Her feet were sheathed in an expensive-looking pair of red and white shoes that sponged the concrete's tears, leaving the coloring muddied. She continued on into the illumination as he mirrored her movements in the darkness.

He stumbled as a small lake in a pothole consumed his ankle. He sighed, rolling up drenched denim that clung to his leg before beginning the trek back to his dorm, head still craned groundward. He halted suddenly before spinning around and gazing once more at that entrance to the building. Oakley's building. Wobbling drunkenly, he used his new-found courage to push himself forward, clambering up the steps in dizzy disarray until he knocked on their door.

"To me, you are poetry. A fearless pursuit in the eye of imperfection to clamber together enough parts to surpass a mortal frame. To me, you are poetry. The cascading freedom of ensnaring the clouds and levitating in their wake. Holding onto nothing to grasp everything. That's it, Oak, that's you."

"That's the problem, Atari. You can't hold anyone to those expectations. Those standards. Do you know how crippling that is, how suffocating it is to be put on such a...a fucking pedestal all the time?"

"It's not a pedestal...it's you—"

"It's the me in your head, Atari. The *'me'* that I've been trying to force myself to live up to for a while now. I can't do this anymore. Now go home, you're drunk." He wobbled backwards as Oakley pushed lightly on his chest, his shaking legs barely able to take the movement as his vision slurred.

A simple yet voracious, "I love you," exploded out of his trembling lips as he fought to keep his words steady. The stench of some cheap vodka he had explored the bottom of still resting upon his tongue. "Oak, just listen to me—"

Oakley raised his voice, his arms tugging the hair from his face in an exasperated movement as he nearly screamed, "Enough of the backwater Kafka act. I'm tired of it, Atari. I'm tired of you. No poem is going to bring you what you want from this, from us. You're trying to force it again. You promised you wouldn't do this."

Atari passed the doorway, gazing longingly around the room as if he'd be taking in every detail for the last time, desperately trying to memorize every nook and cranny. He shot Oakley one last glance, eyes welling with tears, and pleaded, "Oak, I really do love you."

"You don't love me! You don't! We've been together for weeks, Atari. Weeks. Not months. Not years. Weeks." He shook his head, swallowing hard. "No, you don't love me. You're forcing yourself to believe you do because you're so fucking scared of being alone that you'd rather throw yourself at the first person that shows you any sort of interest than spend just one second contemplating why you can't deal with yourself. I'm done."

He eyed Atari down suspiciously, uttering, "Please, just don't do anything stupid. Take care of yourself, get the help you need. Now leave." Oakley scooped up a handful of various clothes and pushed them into his hands, slamming the door behind him so Atari was left in the dorm's hallway in an existence entirely of his own.

He stood there, considering screaming through the wooden door until his lungs shriveled, not bothering to care which neighbors he'd be waking. He thought about bursting through the door, throwing his things down and refusing to leave until they worked things out. His hand raised, ready to knock when he got enough sense to turn around and stumble down the hall, the alcohol in his gut sloshing violently around.

Oakley's words echoed throughout his mind, "Get the help you need," and he opened his phone, flipping through his contacts until his finger hovered over a single name. Emily. He sighed, building up the courage to scroll down his contact list to the name, "Trigger."

"Hey, Trigs, man? You there?"

2

—·—

IMPULSIVE SELF-DESTRUCTION

PRESENT

"SHOTS! SHOTS! SHOTS! SHOTS! Shots!" Cass chanted, shaking her fists through the air like a participant at a sports game. Atari took a long breath, holding the glass to his lips for a second, preparing before swigging the liquor. It burned with a radiance he had grown to love from years of partying. He belched, slamming the glass upon the table where his sloppy hand banged it against the collection of empty glasses already set before him. He giggled, amused by his own drunkenness as his body gave in to the slight sway he was rhythmically trapped in.

"Alright, where is she?" he slurred. Someone passed him a thin glass cylinder, which he held up to his mouth, pulling the weed into his lungs.

He was about to exhale when Annabelle began yelling, "Into the diffuser! Use the diffuser!" She thrust a bottle with a rag in it at him, forcing it into his face as he gagged and struggled to keep the smoke from billowing out. He held the bottle to his lips, puffing out and coughing into the air like a cat hacking up a fur ball, as his singed throat fought for the cooling rush of air.

"I'm- sorry- Anna," he croaked between coughing fits.

Annabelle merely laughed, "It's fine. We just don't want Butchy getting a contact high."

Butch, her new boyfriend, grumbled something under his breath, causing Annabelle to shoot him a glance like she was about to start a fight.

Atari interjected before things got ugly, "Hold up, has anyone seen Trigger?"

"Bathroom," Gal responded in a brief moment of verbal lucidity that showcased he was still there.

Atari wobbled to his feet, legs quivering in a drunken slosh as he excused himself from the room, fighting off the dimming that had sprouted around the corner of his eyes. He made his trek through the hall, hearing Butch pop in with, "So what kinda name is Trigger, anyway?"

Trigger. Thomas. Atari's closest friend had named himself after the video games they used to play. The whole group did, really. All except for Annabelle, who had always refused nicknames besides the occasional bog standard, "Anna." Atari's was easy. Simple. On the nose even. Trigger was for Chrono Trigger. Cass for Dreamcast. Gal for Galaga. Atari's brain fired off the typical response, only realizing his mouth wasn't moving when Annabelle went to transcribe for him. So he continued to the bathroom, rapping his knuckles against the door as he called out, "Trigger? You dead man?"

No response. "Hey Trigger! I swear if you Elvis-ed yourself in Anna's house, she's gonna be pissed!" He creaked the door open.

Trigger stood at the sink, cutting lines of gunpowder with his credit card before dipping in to snort a large section. Atari placed a hand on his shoulder, and he jumped.

"What the hell, man?" Trigger squealed.

"Trigs, I don't think that's what Anna meant when she said we'd be partying. Butch is barely allowing the weed."

Trigger kicked the door shut behind them, bending down and bumping another line. "And that, my friend, is precisely why the bathroom comes in handy. What Butchy doesn't know won't hurt him. And besides," he jiggled something in his pocket, "I have a little surprise for Golden Boy in here too, if you care to indulge?"

Atari's delayed brain took a moment to process a sarcastic response, finally opening his mouth to spit it when something flew at him. He caught it, looking into his hand, and found an unmarked bottle with a few pills in it. "The fuck are these?"

Trigger shrugged. "You don't gotta take it, but my plug assured me it's pretty primo shit. She called it Kronos, but when I looked it up, nothing went by that street name."

Atari eyed down the canister suspiciously. "What's it supposed to do?"

"For how much I paid for it, shit better cure our every waking ailment." He snorted dramatically, rubbing his hand along his nose to wipe off the last of the powder. "Come on, would I ever lead you astray?" he innocently asked. Trigger broke open the bottle, taking a pill and rolling it between his fingers before popping it in his mouth and swallowing it with some sink water.

"You're a pusher, you know that? But how can I say no to a little excitement, especially after the fucking day I had?"

Atari took the bottle, dropping a single pill into his hand. It was a color he had never seen nor could describe and it felt flakey in his hand, as though it would dissolve on his tongue if he left it on there long enough. He pressed the pill into his mouth and held it in his cheek, reached for some water from the sink and gulped it down.

Pain. An immediate, endless pain. He felt it move its way down his throat like a hundred-pound weight had been shoved down his gullet, rapidly expanding his throat muscles as they fought to get away from the agonizing burn. He felt his neck break. His chest exploded. His organs ripped to shreds in a single moment as his soul briefly left his body. And then the next moment he was back inside himself, gasping for air.

"The fuck did you give me, Trigs?" he whimpered. "Trigs?" He looked over to where Trigger's head laid, slumped into the sink and rubbed into the powder like clown makeup. "Trigger man, you alright?" His own words echoed, pounding through his ears seconds after he said them, and he tentatively reached a hand towards his friend. Time collapsed in on itself, a static shift from a slowed lull to extreme speed as if his hand had to push past jelly to get to him.

The world around him shattered as he saw his hand reach out once more, that same hand somehow already holding onto Trigger's shirt moments before he felt its cotton as dozens of hands converged in the center of different intervals, showing each step of the movement individually and somehow all at the same time. He looked around and noticed everything he saw was reflected by the same multitude of itself, like some funhouse glass showing the same thing repeated over and over in a flurry of reflections, only each one seemed to be running on its own time frame, some pushing much faster while others chugged along much slower than the others. Each second was like a slide of a roll of film, all laid on top of each other so one bled into the next.

His body slid between the movement arches, the world melting away into a bedroom as he fought to regain his footing on a new floor. He stood, overlooking the bed back at his place as his eyes fought off the glaze of perception warping. A wiggling mass in the bed drew his eyes, and he watched a blonde girl peek out from under the covers, cloaking her bare chest in his blanket as it draped over her curves.

"Where you goin'? she muttered sheepishly.

"Who are you?" he wanted to say. But his lips moved of their own accord. "Just going out for a smoke, go back to sleep. I'll be back shortly," he said. His hand moved in equally alien autonomy, lunging for a packet of cigarettes by the door. Since when did he smoke cigarettes? He shut the door quietly, heading down the hall and outside into the crisp autumn air. He struck his lighter, putting the cigarette between his teeth and lighting it in one swift and practiced motion. He screamed at his body to stop. To return to his control. But he found himself unable to do anything to stop it. He felt his body preparing to inhale when a car pulled up in front of him.

It was a flaming red '57 Bel-Air, recently polished, reflecting his distorted face as it screeched to a halt. His skin was much older, the crow's feet that were just beginning to sprout around his eyes, exemplified by deep crashing trenches. The imprint of laugh lines that cut through his face were much more defined than they had been moments ago. A scar he didn't remember having pierced the bridge of his nose. He stared deep into his reflection until a voice called out to him.

"You just gonna stare or are you gonna hop on in?"

He looked up to see the same blond as earlier, now fully clothed and patting the passenger seat as she eyed him down mischievously.

"Well, come on in, we don't have all day!"

Me? he thought to himself, confused by the request. His body never asked the same question, instead moving into the car with familiarity, running his fingers along its perfect leather interior before suddenly stopping; his hand on the door.

"Wait here, babe," he croaked in a voice much more weighted than his own. As if it had seen years beyond his comprehension. He pivoted, "I'll be right back," before stepping out of the car and running his hand along the brick exterior of the building, caressing it with two fingers. His fingers led the charge, pushing him somewhere even his own mind couldn't follow as he dug his nails into a chunk between two bricks, filing away until the brick dislodged from its spot. He peeled it out, finding a small crevice in the aged building and shoved the lighter into the wall, before, with just as enigmatic hands, putting the brick back and walking back to the car as if nothing had happened.

"What were you doing?" she puffed.

"Nothing babe, let's get heading." He chuckled a bit, something else laying mysteriously on his tongue. Something that hid under the weight of laughter. He went to slam the door shut.

And just like that, his hand held a doorknob instead of a car door, hesitantly testing its weight with a shaky hand. After a while of standing there, he turned the knob, pushing it open and gasping under the scent of decay. He flicked a light by the door, wandering into the foreign house. He looked around, shock morphing into horror as a single body swung from the center of the room, hanging by a rope that snaked its way up a staircase to the railing above. The noose haloed a snapped neck, hidden under layers of wispy hair that covered what he knew to be vacant eyes. His ex. He knew the second he saw her, even through the bloated, bruised disposition of her face, he knew it was her. The body swayed, somehow still impossibly swayed.

Body. That's all he could think. Not Emily, nor a person of any kind. Just a thing. Just a body. A corpse. He panicked, and this time his frame and mind moved in sync as he rushed towards her. But his core still wasn't his own, dancing with the rope in a desperate attempt to untangle it. Her body hit the ground where it didn't rise. He whipped out his phone, calling for an ambulance despite knowing it was far too late as his adrenaline surged bile in his throat.

And then, just as suddenly as it had started, he found himself back within the confines of the bathroom, bellowing into nothing as Trigger called out in a ramble of rushed fear.

"Emily!" Atari choked, grabbing Trigger by the shoulders and pressing tightly against him to stabilize himself. "We have to find Emily!"

"Your ex?" Trigger replied simply, too stunned for his usual string of sarcastic sentiments.

"Everything okay in there?" Annabelle called out from the other side of the door.

"Everything's peachy. Atari is just a little drunk, is all."

Atari burst through the door, practically trampling Annabelle as he grappled for his shoes. "We need to leave now. I need to get home. I- I need to find Emily." He pushed past his own drunken frame, desperately attempting to maneuver a shoelace as it kept slipping from his shaking grasp. "Fuck."

"Trigger, what the hell did you do to him?"

"He just started screaming about Emily. I don't know, man."

Atari shot his friend a glance. "Come on, grab your shit. We don't have time." Time. How did he know what was going to happen? How was he even sure what he saw was real? And yet, somehow, he just knew.

"Atari! Atari, settle down. What the hell is going on here?"

"Trigger gave me a pill...I- I don't know. I saw something. I saw Emily hanging Anna...hanging in her room. I just- I saw it and I need to get to her now."

Annabelle shot a glance at Trigger. "This was supposed to be drinking and weed only, and you're giving him mystery pills?"

Trigger retracted against the wall. "I just...I just wanted to have some fun with my friend."

Her eyes returned to Atari. "Honey, you're tripping on something. That's all. You're just tripping."

"I'm not Anna, or I may be, but that doesn't change what I saw. I saw it. I saw her dead! I saw...the future or something, I have no idea. I know it sounds crazy, but I saw it. Trigger, you took one too. Tell her!"

"I—"

"What did you see, Trigger?" Cass asked skeptically. Atari had forgotten she was even there as she and Gal watched the argument like a ping-pong match. He looked over to where Butch sat, slumped in his chair with his head drooped, dozing off too much to Emch the conversation.

"Tell them, Trigger!"

"I didn't see anything, man. I certainly didn't see your ex, dead or alive. I just...I laid my head down for a second and you started screaming."

"No, no, there's no way. You gotta trust me here, Anna."

He went to grab his coat but was stopped when she reached out for his arm. "I'm trusting you, Atari, but first you gotta trust me that everything will be fine until the morning. Then we'll head back as a group, okay? Nobody here is in any condition to drive. We need to sleep all this shit off and if you still need to, we can get you back to campus by the morning, alright?"

Atari went to argue, to fight for his stance, but the edges of his vision was still blurred around those blackened corners. Reluctantly, he agreed to stay the night, bunking on the floor with the rest of them as they formed a cluster of drunken limbs like some Bosch painting. That night he dreamt about those lifeless eyes, stained with dried tears and popping out of the skull as she swayed soundlessly like Death's pendulum. He watched himself cradle her in his arms. Felt that blending of reality as everything repeated over and over. The past, the present, the future, all conjoined in an endless array of strings that protruded from his being.

3

UNSTABLE RELATIONSHIPS

PAST

ATARI'S DREAMS CAME LIKE a freight train, bouncing between snippets of past events, always whipping back to Emily's body. Hanging there. Just hanging there. His mind snapping every time just to expand once more into the comfort of liquid memories.

"You don't have to love me the entire time we're alive, just promise you'll hold my hand as I die, and pretend you always did," Atari whispered the words into Em's ear, his voice ricocheting off the little hairs in a low growl as she puffed up her chin slightly, extending her neck so the musculature flared out.

"That's beautiful, Adam."

"It's incomplete," he sighed. "It lacks the punch it's supposed to pack... but it's about you."

"I love it- I love you."

"That'll pass," Atari huffed, staring up at the clouds in an attempt to keep her from seeing the goofy smile that crossed his face whenever she said those three mythical words. He was still getting used to it. They had only been dating for the better part of eight months, and it had taken seven of those months to convince her to say such phrases. She held words sacred, loved to relish in their meaning. She wouldn't say an uninvited phrase like that unless she really meant it, never wishing to circumvent its power. Yet still he felt unsure of her commitment to their relationship, blaming a wall he had put up after his past ones had failed.

She rolled over, half on top of him, her fro tickling his nose. Those honey-dipped eyes gazed at him and suddenly it was as if galaxies reflected off them, such blind exuberance that he couldn't help but stare. "It's not something that'll pass, Adam. Years from now, I'll still be thinking about this moment, right here. There's no cure for that- and trust me, I wish there was," she stuck out her tongue at him and he laughed a little.

"I just find it hard to believe someone like you fell for someone like—"

"You? That's the thing, Adam, you may not see it yourself, but I see a million reasons to love you."

"Do you truly think we can do this?"

"Do what?"

"Make this last. Get married. Start a family—"

"Woah, let's make it to a year first there, cowboy." She laughed a little, cutting it off when she realized he wasn't. "Look, I don't know what the future's gonna hold, but nobody does. I just don't want you getting your hopes up if I can't commit to all that. I know you have such big aspirations, Adam, and I love you for that, but some things need to be taken slowly, is all."

"Oh, yeah...no, you're right."

"Come on, Adam, don't be like that. Look, I never thought about this stuff before you. The happy life with growing old and having kids and stuff, that kinda fantasy, never even crossed my mind." She looked down at the scars that peppered her wrists, running a finger along the mountain range of grooves that stained her brown skin.

"I never thought I'd make it this long. I never had plans to, so it's a lot harder for me to think about the future when I never imagined having one. Look, I never wanted to get married before you. I just never had any interest in it. But now," she held her hand up to the sun, her promise ring glittering on her finger as she waved it slightly.

"How about this? We start with a pet, something simple and easy, and then we go from there. We invent our own lives together. How's that sound, baby?"

"Can we at least get a cool animal? Like a tegu."

"Why don't we start with a cat and move to baby Godzillas later in life?"

Atari flashed a smile. "Fine, but I get to name him, Mr. Hisston Churchill."

"I hate you."

4

— • —

PARANOIA

PRESENT

THE RADIO CROAKED ALONG, huffing to be heard over the bramble of squeaks and squeals the old vehicle let out as it raced down the highway, weaving in and out of traffic as they tore along the road as fast as their pitiful van would allow. "Our quaint town was struck by yet another string of murders, as fifteen-year-old Jacob Tate was found in Sunny Acres, having killed four of his friends. Jacob was taken into custody after sustaining a bullet wound and has since pleaded insanity on all accounts. Little is known about the events that transpired, only that his family claim Jacob was of sound mind and body in the days leading up to the event. Witnesses have described him as a star athlete and scholar, expert witnesses studying his files have claimed years of developmental trauma usually associated with schizophrenia. Uncategorized pills were also found at the scene of the crime. Police are urging anyone with any information to come forward—"

Annabelle flipped the station, which exploded with some retro pop track. The pill felt heavy in Atari's stomach, weighing him down in a cyclone of nausea. What the hell had he taken? The world had returned to normal but colors were still muted, a sensation he wasn't sure he'd ever fully get back.

Trigger fiddled nervously with a strand of tape that littered the box he was sitting on, as Cass' hands danced, tapping invisible piano keys. Gal sat quietly and Butch drove. Nobody said much as they went. Atari had made them leave at first light, wasting no time to get out and back to his room at his rural Pennsylvanian college where he had lived for the past six years. Where Emily lived. She was in her final year, two years younger than him, and completing the course on schedule. With her accelerated workload, she'd be done a semester before him.

Annabelle kept staring at him in the mirror, trying not to make it obvious, which just made it more so. "Are you sure about this, Atari?" she finally spoke, catching his eye in the reflection. "It's been two years, and once you go through with this, there's no going back."

"It has been two years," Cass responded. "Why start anything now? You've moved on. That should be enough."

"I'm not trying to rekindle anything here. I saw what I saw. You all know what I saw. I'm not letting that happen. No way in hell." Even as he said it, he knew he was lying to himself. Everything in him yearned for her. The thought of hearing her voice once more sparked so much excitement in him that he couldn't stop his body from twitching. For the first time in a while, he genuinely felt hope, even amidst the fear of what he had seen.

"You don't have to save everybody, Atari. Not everybody deserves you."

"I have to, with her. Guys, it's- it's Emily. She's in danger...she needs me."

"So, what are you gonna do? I mean, have you even thought this through? You can't just appear at her dorm and say, 'Hey, I took some pills and saw you die'. That'd be crazy," Cass responded.

"I'll figure it out when I see her. For now, we just need to get back to her before it's too late."

Eventually, his head lulled against the van's wall, slowly falling asleep to the thrumming of the engine, only waking again when they had made it back to where his college sat. An uncomfortable air filled the campus, the lingering effects of a place he didn't want to be, especially now that it had all but emptied for Thanksgiving. He parted ways with his friends, his body eclipsing a familiar trek from his dorm room to hers, one he hadn't taken in almost two years, yet held a nostalgic air of excitement as if his body didn't yet understand that his destination wouldn't end with sex and a movie.

A car drove by, and he found himself hypnotized by the rev of its engine, feeling that familiar tugging that nearly forced his body into the road, to jump in front of the car and surrender himself to fate. He could taste the hood, could feel his bones collapse around it, cracking and splintering in a fearful lust that followed him everywhere he went.

He dissociated into this vision, not even realizing he had walked inside until he was standing directly in front of a dorm room marked by two butterflies with the names "Emily" and "Sabrina" branded upon them. Emily's handwriting was sloppy, inconsistent and heavy-handed. Meanwhile, Sabrina rested in an almost gothic aesthetic. He wrapped his fingers around the door, his heart exploding into a million fireworks in his chest.

The door pounced open, flooding the hall with a purple glow as Sabrina stood there, her lazy stance gently backlit.. Her glazed eyes wobbled over him as he tried not to retract into the hallway. "The hell are you doing here?"

"Who's out there, Sabrina?" a voice called out and Atari felt bile rise in his throat, his heart fluttering at the sheer beauty of the voice.

"It's not booze," Sabrina's voice slurred.

"Then who is it?"

"Someone with the wrong room," Sabrina went to close the door, but Atari interjected.

"I need to speak to Emily, please. It's important."

Sabrina slammed the door, and Atari's heart sank. He waited, then waited some more, hearing voices on the other side, but couldn't make out what they were saying. Why was he here? What the hell was he doing? He turned to leave when the door opened once more.

Emily stood in the doorway, her face filled with a combination of anger and confusion. "What the fuck are you doing here, Adam?"

Seeing her now, Atari's voice abandoned him, his throat sinking to the point of near vomiting as he just stared at her. Her gorgeous, split toned lips crashed between a purplish hue and a dark pink. Her wide frown mixed with squinting eyes that ran a honey dipped brown. Her hair had changed, cut a few inches shorter than it had been when they were together, and her light browned skin mixed with the purple light in an intoxicating swirl.

"Huh? You gonna say something, Adam?"

"It's not Adam anymore, it's Atari now...officially," he responded faster than he could think.

"It's officially time for you to get the fuck off my doorstep. I told you not to contact me anymore."

"Em, it's not like that—"

"It's Emily, and I don't care what it is like."

"Emily, please just listen to me. I need to talk to you."

"She said leave, creep," Sabrina interjected from somewhere within the room.

"Sabrina please!" Her slender fingers rapped her temple, decadent multi-colored nails tapping furiously. She sighed, "Look, Adam, I don't care what this is about. You need to move on, hun, I'm telling you, please stop contacting me. I thought we were done with this. I've moved on. I need you to understand that."

Vomit came dangerously close to crashing over the limit. Atari, in full panic mode now, knew he had to speak before it was released. "If you'd just listen to me—"

"Go...home...Adam. Go home. Spend time with your family. Move on. It'll be best for you." She slammed the door and this time, he knew it wouldn't reopen.

He stormed out of the suite, making his way back to the car, and yanked the door open. "Trigger, give me another fucking pill."

"Atari, what happened?" Annabelle pleaded, but Atari could only see red as rage and hurt flooded his senses.

"Just give me another one."

"Atari, we don't even know what this stuff is doing to you."

"I don't care."

"Just listen to us, please," Cass croaked.

"I don't care! I don't...I don't fucking care. Emily is in trouble and I'm the only one that can save her!" Atari was screaming now. He knew he was, but he couldn't stop himself.

He snatched a pill from Trigger's outstretched hand, closing it in his fingers before dry swallowing it. The pain tore through his throat once more, caustically burning in pressure waves that nearly threw him off his feet. His eyes watered, and his nose leaked as the poison entered his body. Immediately, his world dimmed. A black haze rolling over his eyes like oil that obscured his vision, vignetting the car and its passengers as they warily stared at him.

He stomped through the eruption of agony that permeated his every sense as the pill took hold, only subsiding when he thought his mental state was about to shatter completely. The pills' effects were much worse sober, and its influence much stronger as the world blurred again, every possible second visible to him once more. His arm moved, and a string of arms followed at various stages of acceleration and delay, tracking the same exact movement at different intervals. He watched his friends as they thrummed like a long exposure shot from a camera, shaking into the miniscule movements like blinking, muscles twitching in such exuberance it was sickening.

Trigger sat up, bursting from himself like a cicada coming out of its shell. Several versions pulsated to life while others sat in wait, remaining completely still. Atari shifted, fiddling with his senses as he acclimated to the new reality and forced his way deeper, allowing the drugs to take over his mind completely. He slipped between the cracks of time, his vision giving out entirely, and when he came to, he was back on campus, waiting outside Emily's dorm.

At first Atari thought the pills had no effect on him this time, until he realized that everything outside his peripherals faded into abstract nothingness, grooming the surroundings as they fell off into the void. His fingers moved of their own accord once more, working their way into his hair as he ruffled it up slightly, pushing what appeared to be a hodgepodge of several hairstyles at once into something more presentable, as he stared at his mirrored self in the doorknob. His body motioned for the door. His hands were shaking.

Inside was a long stretch of hallway, stretched to mock infinity by the way his legs buckled underneath him. He traced the floor with his eyes, never raising them as he shuffled down the length of the catacombs, not stopping his snail's assault until he reached the door marked by the butterfly branded "Emily."

He went to knock on the door when it flung open before he could. The scent of a candle invaded his nose immediately, the same smell he had experienced the first time around as he found his nostrils exploring the foreign invader. Caramel, with a hint of pine trees. The second thing he noticed was the pulsating purple light that flooded the hall with an ethereal glow, speckling his clothes and skin. The third thing, the person standing in the doorway.

She was small. Short and thin, with an odd set of proportions that looked like it was cobbled together from multiple bodies at once. Endless legs formed the base. Spindly brown tree trunks that curved only slightly at the thigh, caught within the trapping of a porn-star plaid skirt with a studded belt that connected them to her stumpy torso. Her chest was nearly completely flat, a curt wave that rippled her shirts just slightly even with the support of a bra, so much so it was almost lost completely under her leather jacket. She carried a whimsical sense to her, like a woodland Fae, with her long, curly hair brushed against prodding ears, poofing out into a majestic mane-like fro.

"Well, are you gonna stare or are you gonna come on in?" she demanded, her voice fluttering in an airy breeze like a spoken word poet.

"Is that an offer?" he winked, giving the innuendo a second to settle in.

She laughed, stepping back slightly so he could enter the room. "Maybe if you're lucky. So, what are we watching tonight?"

"It's gotta be horror, right? Something scary but in a 'you'll wanna fuck me later', kinda way. So no gross outs. Something snuggly."

"You thinking what I'm thinking?"

"Depends. Are you thinking academy award winner M. Night Shyamalan's hit movie 'Signs'?"

She plopped down on the bed, giggling to herself as her hair bounced from the impact. "It's already in the DVD player. Just flick the button."

"You really already had it in? Am I becoming that predictable?"

"What can I say besides," her voice deepened, caught in the mocking of a gruff exterior, "'Nothing can stop us from enjoying this movie, so enjoy it!'"

They laughed, curling up on the bed together and wrapping their arms around one another. Atari looked at her, so content in the memory he had forgotten he wasn't really there until the edges faded. He fought it, concentrating hard on her face and forgetting about his mission as he studied her every curve. Bliss! She could only be described as a cartoonish sense of bliss. He focused intently on her eyes until scenery materialized through them as they faded into fog, growing ever more translucent, his mind momentarily sinking into a black pit before re-emerging within a sputter of white.

Blackness. Whiteness. The cycle was nauseating, but he was starting to get used to the feeling. Something was different this time. When he came out of that blinding flash of white light, he was met by darkness once more. He moved his head, actually moved it as though he was back in control and he wondered if the pills had worn off and taken with them his vision.

Only he couldn't feel his hands. He tried to move, but it was as though there was nothing to move at all. He found his essence moving forward. Not his body. Not even really moving at all. Just a tugging at his very being, like he was being pulled down with the intense gravitational rush of a rollercoaster ride. A figure loomed off in the distance, permeating the utter blankness that surrounded it. The figure expanded, growing larger and larger as if he were approaching it, and as it came into being, he could make out a huddled over body.

The body of Emily sat before him, hunched against the void. She was nude, her shoulder blades distended. The bones pierced the skin as if wrapped around a frame several sizes too small.

She shivered; pencil-thin arms wrapped around her stubborn frame like she was trying to cloak herself in the surrounding darkness. Atari found his spirit rounding Emily, and immediately wished he hadn't.

The mock face was slender. Brown. With no beginning or end, instead stretching indefinitely, on an unnaturally smooth surface that neither belted nor concaved. He watched, unable to maintain any semblance of self-preservation as his ex's body expanded, the skin constricting the bones, a bowstring on the verge of snapping. Each limb expanded out into the void, entirely consuming his vision in flesh. Only when his mind's comprehension was threatening to snap did he wake up, body pressed against the concrete as a round of screaming circled him, coming from multiple directions at once.

5

— · —

Self-harm

Present

"You fucking killed him, Trigger. You fucking killed him."

"Did you see the way he was looking at me? There was no saying no to giving him the damn pills."

"And who bought the fucking pills, Trigger? It was supposed to be a weed and drinking only party, not some, 'hey, I'll do fucking coke then give my friend mystery drugs' type party."

"I love Atari just as much as you assholes. I'd never do anything to hurt him—"

"Guys?"

"My dealer's reputable. I didn't pull this one off the street. Her mom's a doctor."

"Guys!"

"Oh good, so your dealer steals shit from her own mother! And you just, what? Trust her with that shit?"

"Guys, he's moving!"

Atari's mind wavered, unable to parse out who was saying what as consciousness hit him like a professional boxer. His eyes rolled around to the feet of those around him, watching them pace, or tap, or lock in place. His fingers twitched, attempting to close around anything he could use to ground himself, and he bordered dangerously on vomiting. Finally, with a sharp intake of breath, life reclaimed him. His body curled into action, painstakingly rising to his knees and then to his feet as he drew in a fresh breath of air.

His mouth was bone dry, juxtaposing his clammy skin that dripped with a perfuse coating of sweat. He was alive; he knew he was alive, but his body felt catatonic, like it was still in a state of sleep even as he moved around. His brain began to take in more of his surroundings. The beating sun pressed onto everyone's skin; shadows stuck in the same exact position as if only a minute had passed.

Atari's head wobbled on an axis, the world drunkenly dancing by his eyes on delayed intervals. He shivered, his body convulsing slightly. The pills were damaging his body. He could feel the after-effects lingering on his stubborn frame. He went to speak when something off in the distance caught his eye. Outcropping from some enigmatic corner space between two buildings, captivated in shadow, was a great, fleshy mass.

Its features were entirely blurred, some ethereal glass blocking any distinctive traits, but the mass was unmistakably the creature from his dreams. Its slender, placid, palm tree of a body reaching a height of at least fifteen feet. Two spindly arms, skeletal with a thin layer of ill-fitting skin, being the only bridge between knobby bones, any semblance of muscle tissue entirely absent. It looked as if someone had taken the skin of a child and stretched it to fit the frame of a giant. It didn't move so much as it glimmered in ethereal waves like a mirage in a cartoon. He stared at it and could feel it staring back despite its face being an entirely blank slate. His eyes locked for an unknown amount of time before Cass's voice drew him back to reality.

"And you're staring at...what exactly? Trigger, I think you fucked up his brain."

"His brain was stubbornly clinging to a concoction of liquor and Vicodin before he was exposed to anything I gave him," Trigger wailed, desperation wrapping tight to each syllable.

Gal's eyes bounced back and forth between the two as they bickered, every once in a while, flickering to Atari and giving him a gentle smile. He was the first to offer Atari a hand, holding him steady as his shaky legs threatened a total collapse.

Butch circled the van, and as he came into view Atari realized for the first time that he had been absent. "What's with all the yelling?" Butch pressed.

"Nothing, hun, Atari just tripped is all," Anna stated firmly, waiting for any of the others to challenge her as she let her body fall into his embrace, leaning into his chest.

Butch wasn't convinced. His eyes scanned Atari. "You look like death."

Atari's eyes flickered between Butch and the looming presence of the great creature. "I'm fine...just need some rest is all. Yeah, that's all...just been a day." As his head was beginning to clear, he once again realized how much of an ass he had made of himself in front of Emily.

Annabelle took his shaking hand, caressing it slowly, and Butch's face soured slightly in Atari's peripherals. "You need to sleep things off," she cooed in a motherly voice. "But you also can't be alone right now. Not while those drugs are in your system, not while you're weak. One of us should stay with you, I'll—"

"I'll do it," a voice interjected. All eyes turned towards Trigger, whose hand was half raised like he was in a classroom. His eyes darted between them, daring each individual to challenge him.

"I'm not sure if that's such a good idea," Annabelle croaked.

"Anna...trust me...please." Trigger shifted awkwardly, his defiance seeming to falter as he gazed into her eyes, something adjacent to sorry reflecting from his own. "I'm not going to do anything...I'm not going to fuck this up any further. It should be me. Besides, for better or worse, I have the most experience with come-offs. It has to be me."

Atari was taken aback by the seriousness of Trigger's voice, a rare moment of lucidity he wasn't used to his friend expressing. Annabelle must've felt the same because her resolve floundered, surrendering to his request with a simple, "Okay."

They watched as Trigger and Atari left, Atari still stumbling a little as the world around him was trapped in a perpetual tumble. He stumbled all the way back to his dorm room; the walk seeming to take ages and seconds all the same as time became irrelevant. He didn't notice that Trigger had been uncharacteristically silent until he was within the confines of the dorm, plopping on the couch and staring at Trigger's dour face. He contemplated prodding when Trigger pulled up a chair, sitting in it like he was about to give a seminar, then letting out an elongated sigh.

"I lied."

Atari's thick eyebrows furrowed in confusion as he quizzically stared at his friend's gruff disposition. "What?"

"About not seeing anything. While you were under. While we were under. I lied. I'm sorry?"

"Trigger, are you—"

"No, no, I'm not," he licked his lips, his eyes boring such a deep sorrow that Atari had never seen on his friend's face before. He was certainly not okay. Trigger gave a little nod, as if hyping himself up to speak. "When we took the drugs. I remember watching you take them. Closing my eyes. And seeing her. Luna. It was three days before her..." his voice trailed off into a pained silence. "It was three days before. We were together, driving. It was night, and alongside the road, she saw a bunch of sheep behind a fence. You know how much she loved animals. She got all excited. She's pointing them out to me and giving them these goofy little names. You know, she's Luna."

He was rocking in the chair, teetering on unstable legs as he continuously wiped his palms on his jeans, as if trying to rub off the very layer of skin that covered them. "Only she spots something along the fence and makes me stop the car. Screams, literally screams at me until I stop. She's flinging herself out the door before the car's even in park, and I forget to put on my blinkers as I'm rushing to catch up with her. A sheep must've gotten stuck in the fence. Its legs were mangled, twisted in knots from its desperate attempts to get out. It was bleating. Calling for help, she said. She ran over and I knew from the second I saw it she wasn't leaving until we had helped it. It took us an hour of pulling and shoving and creative thinking to get this fucking sheep out of this fence. All the while, it's screaming and kicking at us and throwing up mud from the rain. We're getting filthy, but you know Luna. She's unrelenting. We finally, finally, after all this effort, get the damned thing free, and it drags itself off on injured legs, prancing off without so much as a thank you."

He paused his story to give the most forced, unenthusiastic echo chamber of his usual laugh. "She was so proud; her eyes were gleaming. She went to return to the car and...another car, they...it was dark. We were on a bend, parked where we shouldn't have been, and I never turned those damned flashers on...it was over before I knew it, before I could process anything that was even going to happen. The driver had to call an ambulance...I couldn't even do that. Not for my own sister...I couldn't." His head shaking had become more feverish. His palms rubbing so violently Atari was scared he'd begin to get brush burn, but he sat quietly and listened. "I knew she was gone then, at that very moment, before the man had even called. When her poor body hit the ground..." He sighed. "Three days...it was three days later that she..."

"But I saw all that. And I see that a lot, I hear it a lot. Constantly." His eyes met Atari's for the first time since his monologue began. "Never before has it been that vivid. That...just...like the day it had happened, more so even maybe. Like I felt every last second in reality. Only I had no control over my body, everything was...predestined. I thought I was trapped there, reliving those three days, and then something happened. I saw this black being out of the corner of my eye. It was huge, lingering, just that...just lingering there. I don't know what I saw, Atari, but I've never been so scared. That thing, I couldn't even stare at it because I still wasn't in control of my body. But its energy radiated, malignant, vile. Like it could see into my head and was feeding off my reaction to my sister's..."

"Then I heard you screaming, and I came to and I was back in the bathroom. I couldn't tell the others, I just couldn't. They don't need to see that side of me. Nobody should. That's not the Trigger they know." He gave a half-hearted smile, which quickly faded. "I thought it was like a bad acid trip. Until I saw it again outside after you took those pills and woke up the second time. And even more so after I realized you saw it, too. You did see it! Don't play it like you haven't. I saw it in your eyes."

Atari remained quiet for an extended minute, taking in all this information. The pills, what they made Trigger see, sounded exactly like what he had experienced. He had never heard his friend discuss what had happened to his sister. An enigmatic cloud of mist always surrounded the topic from the second it had happened. Trigger had never broken down, never cried before now. But now he watched his friend weep, tears streaming down a face that had never heralded them before. It was odd, disjointed, even more of an abstract concept than the creature itself.

The creature. If Trigger had seen it too, then it validated what had been creeping inside Atari from the moment he had laid eyes on it. It was real. Atari motioned to put a hand on Trigger's shoulder, who shrugged off the physical contact immediately. "It's fine. I'm fine." He stifled a sob, which got lodged in his throat. "I just didn't want the others to know. I'm scared, Atari. I don't know why or what I had us take, but I'm scared."

Atari went to comfort his friend, to reassure him that everything would be okay, but when he opened his mouth, his response was a simple, "Me too."

"I fucked up...yet again, I fucked up."

6

EXTREME EMOTIONAL SWINGS

PRESENT

TRIGGER'S BODY JOLTED AWAKE as he began to slide off the chair, catching himself in a stuttering, sleep deprived state. He looked over at Atari, who was sleeping off the intoxication on the couch, snoring a bit as his chest heaved. Trigger stood on shaky legs, wandering over to the slumped body on the couch. The power must've gone out, as the lights they had left on were no longer illuminated.

"Hey, psst, Atari? Hey man?" He shook Atari's arm a bit, making sure he was still breathing. He had dealt with one too many ODs and knew he had to check on his friend every so often. "Adam?"

Atari didn't budge. Trigger sighed. He had to piss, so he decided to go ahead with that plan and try waking up Atari afterwards. He began his trek down the hall, lit only by the glow of his phone. He went to the decrepit dorm room bathroom, pissing into the bowl and washing his hands. He splashed water on his face, desperately trying to shake the drug addled slumber from his eyes. Two days later and he was still feeling the effects of the pills. How they shaped the outline of his stomach, cramping it with emptiness. How they split his head. How they threw off his balance.

He looked into the mirror. His nose was an ax, chopping the air before it in an aerodynamic twist only hindered by its slight curve to the left. His hair danced around before his eyes, bangs shielding his elongated forehead from view and his cheeks began at boney points, sloping drastically into a defined chin. He was like a collage of handsome parts thrown into a blender where they created a hodgepodge mess that never knew what to replicate.

He slapped the darkness, fumbling his hand for the knob when he was hit by a sudden uneasy queasiness. He contemplated heading back to the toilet to vomit, but tried shoving it down as he turned the knob and escaped through the bathroom door. The hallway was caught in an endless trail of darkness, like someone had carpeted the floor and walls in the night sky. Such a pitch black that it ate away at the light emanating from his phone. He began walking, a slow trek through curtains of nothingness as he let the small light guide him. Step after step seemed to only take him further into the enigmatic maws of charcoal air.

"Atari?" he called out, confused as to why he hadn't made it back to the living room yet. The hall hadn't been that long, no more than a dozen steps, but he just kept going, further and further into the darkness.

Step after step after step. Further and further down the hall. He turned around, but the bathroom was nowhere in sight anymore, the hall instead stretching infinitely in that direction as well. Each rapid turnover bled into the next as his legs grew tired from the hours of descent. His body pushing on by fear alone as he struggled to push through the suffocating waves of gloom. "Atari?"

Something answered. Not a voice but a squeal like an old car screeching to a stop permeated his senses, folding dangerously against his ears.. Then the screaming started. Even in the wake of the blood-curdling howls of pain, Trigger could easily identify the source as his sister. Luna bellowed like an animal, her voice coming from every direction at once, and Trigger found himself taking off at a sprint, ignoring the threat of walls as he raced onward. "Luna? Luna!"

He found himself consumed by a blinding light, erratically exploding into being as he came to a clearing where a road took a drastic bend around a cliff side. That road. His heart fluttered as his eyes grazed the ground, coming to where a mangled body lay, pressed into the concrete, in a pond of their own blood. Luna's body laid there, the car having already disappeared, leaving behind only the tread marks to showcase its attempt to slow.

Trigger found himself inching towards the scene, too afraid to look directly at it as he side-eyed the crimson splatter. He gagged as the scent hit him, plugging his nostrils in a thick haze of rot. He had to turn away as his head began swaying, vision blurring into his own panic, when the crunching of bones began clicking in his ears. He turned, facing the body for the first time when it began moving, a gradual inflation of both arms as they bent around destroyed bones. Then suddenly her chest rose into the air as if hoisted by strings, ribcage snapping like flames off a campfire as it bent impossibly, her shattered neck lolling to the side.

The body rose on all four limbs, twisting around and scurrying towards him as Trigger squealed, racing into the endless void. A wave of noise crashed over his ears, pulsating throughout his skull as it wrapped around his screams, dragging his senses through stinging blades. He ran until his legs could go no further, careening through spirals of silky black nothingness, the sound of bones scraping and cars rushing to slam brakes still permeating the air.

Then, just as suddenly as he had left it, he found himself back within the hallway, still toting his phone like a flashlight and walking down its length as if nothing had happened. For a brief second of bliss, he thought he had just been through a bad trip, nothing more, nothing less, just a drug fueled nightmare that had trapped him. That was, until he rounded the corner into what should've taken him back to the bathroom, and his eyes felt like they were going to melt out of his skull.

Standing in the dim light of the window was a withering mass, wobbling on two legs like an idle fighting game character. From the hip down it was normal, and from the neck up it bore a striking resemblance to his sister Luna, only showcasing inconsistencies through its dull, lifeless eyes. Everything in between was a Bosch painting of a surrealist nightmare, as dozens of limbs skewered her nude body in various directions, all of which withered and writhed at different speeds and patterns.

The Hecatonchires-esque beast took a step forward, gallivanting towards him as Trigger let out a pathetic squeal. He turned to run, but the air had trapped him, turning solid as if walls were pushing in on all sides except for where the creature approached. Trigger squirmed, pushing his shoulders out and forcing his muscles to expand as the invisible walls grew tighter, squeezing him into a box.

The Hecatonchires took another step forward, then another, clearing the distance between them easily. The largest of its arms reached out, pinning Trigger against the void. He cried out to anyone that would hear. Its countless hands folded over Trigger's body, groping his flesh as they snaked across his curvature. A hungry, sensual touch Trigger was far too familiar with. Each hand slithered over his frame, getting more aggressive with its grip until the pain boiled his body alive. He looked down.

The hands were tearing at his skin, fingers ripping flesh from muscle as they snaked beneath the skin. Trigger howled. His sister's face silently stared at him, devoid of emotion. An arm that cropped through her breast reached up, driving through the skin of his neck, and he could feel veins shift, the hand vibrating to match the frequency of his screams.

The mangled visage of his sister began melting, seeping inside the open wounds that coated his body, mixing with blood and pulsating muscle. He watched helplessly as his body absorbed her until there was nothing left of the beast. He sighed. His heart was racing, consuming his entire chest. He looked down, and as he did so, he realized his body was moving of its own accord, no longer restrained by the invisible walls.

His feet marched over to the counter, a performative stride that overcame the distance in a few short bounds. He took one last look in his mirror, where his haunting face carried a new presence. One that those hodgepodge of mismatched features didn't know they could evolve into. He gazed into his own eyes. Weeping. A weeping and silent void as they swayed closer, driving his face into the glass where it shattered into dozens of icicles of various sizes. He watched helplessly as his arms moved, grabbing for a particularly large piece, gripping it so tight that his palm and fingers began to bleed. He eyed the piece, quivering within himself as his mind contemplated all the damage it could do. Then, in one swift motion, he began to carve.

His hand twitched, stabbing into his forearm and dragging the piece of glass all the way up his wrist.

The muscle fought to stop the blade, but his diligent hand was stronger, forcing it so deep he could feel it scraping the bone. Then he pulled it out, watching blood seep into the carpet below, and began on his other arm. Where he expected pain, expected agony, he was met by nothing. An absolute, all-consuming, nothing. He dropped the makeshift blade, eyes glued to the damage he had done. Both wrists were slashed, geysers of crimson leaking from the wounds in great spurts. His vision was already beginning to darken, existence plummeting around him as his senses abandoned him. He didn't scream or cry, he just let the nothingness wash over him like a warm blanket.

7

—·—

Chronic Emptiness

Present

ATARI AWOKE TO THIN beams of light from the living room window peppering his face, washing into his eyes and giving him that comfortably warm sense of peace. He rolled over, contemplating pulling the blankets up over his eyes and going back to sleep, but something felt off. He didn't know if it was the drugs still in his system or what, but the surroundings gave him an uneasy chill.

His eyes fluttered, blinking the sleep away, and he slowly curled himself into a sitting position, looking around the room. A mass of blankets laid haphazardly on the chair beside him, spiraling in a clump as if someone had spent the night cocooned within them. Trigger. Atari bolted upright, yelping his friend's name and waiting for a response.

"Trigs, man. You there?"

No response. He stood, inspecting the room. Nothing. He gazed down the hall. The bathroom light was on, peeking through a door that was slightly ajar. "Trigger? You snorting something, man? It's a little early, don't you think?"

He stumbled down the hall, his legs still liquefied in a sleepy stupor. He crashed through the bathroom door. Trigger laid on the floor, head resting against the bathtub as Adam's apple pierced the sky. Both his wrists had gaping vertical slits slashed into them, blood soaking into the floor around him. "Trigger!"

Atari dove on his knees, checking Trigger's neck for a pulse. There was one, but it was faint, his heartbeat barely registering. Atari scrambled for towels, draping them over the open wounds and applying pressure with one hand while his other fumbled through his pocket for his phone. He called 9-1-1, bellowing into the phone.

———

ATARI RAN HIS FINGERS along the rails of the hospital bed, feeling the rough pattern on the plastic slide across his calloused fingers. He raised his eyes from the floor momentarily, just enough to take in the nest of wires that consumed his friend's frame, various IVs pressing their way under his skin and pumping liquids of multiple tones into his veins. His arms were packaged in gauze, the skin beneath was a revolting blackish-brown, and the largest tube slithered its way into his throat, keeping him breathing.

A tugging on his shoulder pulled Atari back to reality as Cass spun him around, her mouth uttering words that never bypassed the foggy static of Atari's muddled brain. "What?" he said, just as deftly.

She gestured across the room where a doctor stood waiting for a response. "What?" he repeated.

"I said it's important for us to know if he had taken anything prior to admittance. We need to be aware of any potentially harmful mixtures, so we know the proper medications to give him. Your friends say you were the last one to be seen with him, Mr. Adam."

"Atari," he mumbled subconsciously, fingers still twirling around the plastic bed guards. "I don't know."

"Are you sure? It's imperative that we—"

"I don't know, okay! I was asleep. I woke up, and he was like this. I- I don't know."

"Do you know if your friend regularly uses any substances, any at all?"

"What doesn't he use?" Butch scoffed. "Guys a walking meth lab."

"Fuck yourself, Butch," Cass hissed.

"This is just what happens to people like that. He should've been locked up where he couldn't harm himself or others."

"Listen here, you fucking prick, that's our friend you're talking about!" Cass shoved back her chair, standing when Anna stepped between them.

"Jesus fuck guys, calm down. This is a hospital."

"I wasn't—"

"Not another goddamn word, Butch!" She turned towards the doctor. "I'm sorry we're all worried and stressed and nobody's slept. We just need to know if he's going to be okay. He is going to be okay, right?"

The doctor's eyes dropped to the ground for a split second before fluttering back up as if he had caught himself doing it. "There are too many variables at play to make a judgment call so soon. He got most of the right veins, a lot more than most do, and with a clean cut. Your friend lost a lot of blood. He must've been unconscious for hours and with the way he was positioned he cut off circulation to his legs as well. Our best course of action right now is to pump as much blood back into him as we can and hope for the best. His levels are...decent given the situation. Unfortunately, right now all I'm able to tell you is it'll be a waiting game, but for now the meds are keeping him under, so he's not feeling any pain. I'd recommend that you try to stay optimistic."

"That's a crock of shit. What happened? We were just with him. Trigger isn't suicidal. Tell him, Atari!"

"I—"

"Cass, we all know that Thomas hasn't been well since his sister's passing."

"Don't call him that! He hates being called that!"

"He's in a fucking coma. Does it matter what we call him?"

"Guys?"

"He's still here! He can still hear us! He can still hear us, right?"

"That would depend on which scientific circles you follow and applies on a person-by-person basis, but to some degree, yes—"

"See! I told you—"

"Guys!" Atari hollered, silencing the room. Atari looked around the room, taking in the stunned reactions of his friends as well as the doctor. "He took some pills," Atari admitted, eyes wandering just below the doctor's face, obscuring its details. "We don't know what or how many, but that was two days ago. He had some coke, probably some weed. He's on antidepressants... I don't know what else." His head dropped again, staring down at his feet.

"Thank you. I need to go discuss with the team and come up with a game plan." The doctor excused himself from the room, shifting the curtain behind him so it blocked them off from the rest of the ICU wing.

Someone walked up behind Atari, placing a hand on his shoulder, "So you really think he can hear us?"

"I don't know, Anna."

"And he didn't say anything, about- about any of this? No hints or clues or anything?"

Atari sighed, lingering in the silence until Anna continued, "Okay. It's okay, Atari. He's gonna be okay."

Atari's hand slid up, fingers interlocking around Annabelle's. "He didn't do this Anna... I know it sounds crazy, but he wouldn't do this. Not now, not with me around." Atari went quiet, though he knew exactly what he wanted to say. Trigger had taken the drugs, too. It had to be tied to that. Tied to the beast he had seen after he had taken them.

8

— · —

SHIFTING SELF-IMAGE

PRESENT

"ARE WE SURE THIS is such a good idea?"

"Loosen up, Atari, you heard the doctor. This shit's just a waiting game now. What else are we gonna do? Besides, we needed to get out of that sterile hospital for a bit before we went mad and stabbed Butch to death with surgical scissors."

"Can we not talk about him like that, Cass? He's a good man, he's just had a different upbringing than we had, is all. And growing up different from Trigger isn't always a bad thing."

They walked under the bar's flashy neon sign, briefly illuminating the top of their heads, a vibrant mix of purple and orange like a Brandon Woelfel portrait. Atari bounced between the two, interlocking his arms around Cass and Annabelle as Gal trailed off a bit behind them, silent as always as his eyes grazed as much of his surroundings as he could. Butch had stayed home, the bar not really being his scene.

They checked their IDs with the bouncer. Cass, the youngest of the group, was eyed suspiciously before being let in. Her dainty, paper-thin frame and exuberant youthful features mocked that of someone much younger than twenty-one. Once they were granted access, they migrated to an unoccupied booth, sitting and ordering a round of drinks and appetizers.

Atari got his usual two straight shots of bottom shelf vodka, not bothering with the extra cost of the fancier drinks. Liquor was liquor to him, and nothing excited his senses more than the post shot burn pressed against his chest and throat. Under the table, his hand fiddled with the container of mystery pills in his jacket pocket, contemplating sneaking into the bathroom to pop another. Maybe then he'd know how to help his friend.

The table pounded away their first round of drinks, making small talk every so often as nobody knew what to say. An escape. The bar was an escape from the hospital, from their friend's current situation, but how could they escape their own minds? Atari ordered his second round immediately after finishing his first, knowing he'd be draining his pathetic bank account throughout the night. Then a third round, then a fourth, quickly bypassing the rest of the table. Shot glasses accumulated on the table, left behind by inattentive wait staff. Not even an hour in, he was cradling a fourth round of shots, his stomach sloshing as the liquor began dulling his senses.

At a point in the night Atari found himself giggling along to his friends' attempts at playful banter, reciting epics in the shape of their pasts. "Remember, my ex-boyfriend? What was his name again? Not Harold, the one with the somehow less moan-able name."

"Derick?" Cass chimed in, as if reading off a catalog as her eyes flipped from left to right.

"That's the one! The gas lighter! And remember when I caught him cheating, so he threw me out, so then a week or whatever later I'm breaking into his house and stealing his favorite vinyl. Just fully used my key and got in and everything-"

"Trigger wanted him to shave a dick on their cat, too!" Cass gleefully recalled.

"He did!" Annabelle chimed in. "And thank God you didn—"

"I know, right? I totally should've! Trigger always was the big ideas guy." He raised another glass to his lips, the sharp smell of poison invading his senses, but a voice stopped him, causing the hairs on his arms to stand soldier straight.

He slung his head around, the world spinning past his eyes, swaying even after his movement had stopped. Emily sat at the bar, alone, as her finger twirled around the circumference of a shot glass. "Hey barkeep, a lovely lady's looking to die over here tonight," she whistled, getting the attention of a massive man behind the bar. His towering frame was only matched by his equally wide face, pressed into a Viking style beard, the sideburns nearly connecting with bushy eyebrows.

"You ain't drivin' are yuh?" he spat.

"Nope, just wobblin'." She raised a glass to the sky. "Cheers?"

A foot collided with Atari's knee. "What the hell, man?"

"Don't even think about it," Anna hissed. They must've all noticed him staring. "It's bad news."

"She needs to know—"

"She doesn't. You don't even know!"

"Gal, get up."

Gal just looked at him, his eyebrows raising slightly.

"Gal, get up!"

"I don't think that's such a—"

"It's a bad idea, yeah- yeah. I know. Now let me up!"

Gal reluctantly stood aside, allowing Atari to force his way out of the booth. Cass just stared, something close to pain reflecting in her eyes while Anna shook her head disapprovingly.

Atari stumbled his first few steps, the liquor guiding his feet, so they slid like he was walking on ice. What was he doing? Atari attempted to stop himself, to turn back and enjoy the night with his friends, but the liquid courage mixed with his manic state pushed him forward. He wandered over to the bar, pulling back the stool and loudly announcing, "Is this seat taken?"

Emily jumped, her back squaring as the muscles tensed. "You've gotta be fucking me."

"Haven't in a while, actually." He smiled at her, brashly taking pleasure in the way her face soured. Self-destruction had always been a specialty of his.

"Adam, what the fuck?" she hissed.

"Atari."

"I don't care. This whole stalker vibe has gotta go, Adam- Atari, whatever. Whoever."

"I need to talk to you, and I need you to listen. Truly, listen."

"What? What could possibly be so important?" She didn't wear spite well, and Atari could tell she was being intentionally off putting. Even so, he found himself drawn to the way her lips pirouetted, wishing for nothing more than to kiss them. He nearly leaned in, his body instinctively wanting her, craving her.

"It's complicated, but you need to listen-"

"I'm not getting back to you, Atari. I keep telling you, it just wasn't meant to be. It wasn't the right time, or the right person, or the right whatever. The constellations didn't align, and we just weren't meant to be. You have to learn to accept—"

"Trigger slit his wrists..."

Emily stopped, her mouth hanging open. She placed her glass on the table and stared into Atari's eyes for the first time in years. Her eyes were wide, beautiful depths of hazel and countless memories of those wondrous eyes flooded through Atari, intermixed with images of Trigger slung against the bathtub. Finally, she spoke, "I'm so sorry- I know how much he means to you..."

"I thought you should know. I know you two aren't close anymore, but there was a time- I just thought you should know. It's bad, Emily. They don't know if he's gonna make it. He- he- he's attached to all these- these machines, and he lost a lot of blood. There were handprints all over the floor and wall he had crawled around. He had tried to get to me, and I just slept through it. If I had just gotten to him..."

"Look, Adam, none of that is your fault. None of it. I'm sorry this happened to you, and I hope that he pulls through. We all know he's had his issues ever since his sister's passing... since even before then with the things she did to him when they were kids... I don't know what I'm saying, all I know is that you'll be there for him when he wakes up and that's all that matters right now. Now go back to your friends- they need you."

"I can't- I can't face them. Em I- I- fuck, everybody around me is getting sick or dying and every time all I can think is, what if I die and my only thoughts are, 'maybe tomorrow.' Because that's all I think anymore, 'maybe tomorrow I'll find a reason to get out of bed.' Or 'maybe tomorrow I'll finally find that thing that makes me happy.' I can't keep this shit up anymore. I- I can't lose anymore. I can't let you die." He let the last sentence slide from his lips without taking the repercussions into consideration, flinging the sentiment before his brain had even registered what he was saying.

A hand slid from Emily's lap, squeezing his arm. Atari looked down at her hand, squeezing it back, and noticed a tiny collage of doodles speckling her skin almost like constellations. A tiny Kilroy sat on one finger surrounded by even tinier text that read 'Em was here'. All the galaxy's stars blended together with the actual tattoo of a semi-colon on her wrist, one she had gotten long before they were ever together.

"Adam, I'm okay. I'm not planning on dying any-time soon." He looked in her eyes and all he could see was her lifeless body swaying on the rafters, puffy, swollen eyes popping out of her skull as her broken neck displayed a mangled formation. He knew he couldn't let that happen, but what was he supposed to tell her that'd get her to believe? His hand returned to the pills in his pocket, scraping dusty flakes off one pill. If he just gave her one, if he let her see for herself, maybe he'd be able to stop it.

He opened his mouth to speak, to offer up a pill in a last-ditch effort, but something out of the cor-ner of his eye caught his sight. He jumped back-wards, knocking his glass onto the floor, where it shattered. The beast from earlier was lumbering outside the window, under a streetlamp, half its detail-less body illuminated by the light, while the other half remained hidden in shadows.

"What the fuck is that?"

Emily turned her head to follow his eyes, obviously not seeing anything, as she turned back towards him. "Adam, are you on something? If you need a ride to the hospital, I'll cover the cost."

"You don't see it...?"

"See, what? The lamp?"

"I- I- I gotta leave. I'm sorry, I just..." he stumbled off, slamming his hip into the side of a table and nearly toppling a dancing couple as he fought his way outside. As soon as the doors were open, he found that the creature was gone, leaving no trace of its existence besides the memories that flooded his mind. He turned, overwhelmed by a combination of fear and anxiety, and vomited into a bush.

9

—·—

EXPLOSIVE ANGER

PRESENT

"I'M TELLING YOU- IF you'd just believe me—"

"We're trying, Atari, but you're talking about fucking demons here."

"I'm talking about the thing that tried to kill Trigger!"

"Trigger...tried to kill Trigger. And would've if you hadn't been there."

"You heard the doctor; they told us there was no way- no way- that Trigger could've gotten that clean a cut on both wrists on his own. It's just not possible."

"He wasn't there, Atari. You weren't there- shit, I didn't mean it like that."

Atari scoffed, picking up a few paces and kicking a rock in a rage.

"Atari...maybe you should stay with us tonight? You shouldn't be alone right now." Annabelle raced to catch up with him.

"With Butch?"

"Yes, with me and Butch."

"Fuck Butch, Anna. You heard him in there. He'd be fine if Trigger died."

"Atari, you're drunk. You can't even walk in a straight line."

"I'm fine, tell them I'm fine, Gal." A moment of silence as all heads turned towards Gal. Atari flicked his forehead. "Oh, that's right, you're a mute son-of-a-bitch." He flipped his gaze to Gal's solemn eyes and swore he saw the glimmer of something within them for a second. A vacant nothing beyond that of anything he had ever seen before.

"Oi, what'd he ever do to you?"

"Fuck off, Cass."

"Maybe we should all just go home, relax a bit and all that." Annabelle whimpered, side-eyeing Atari, "Cool off."

"My friend is fucking dying. I am cool." Atari took a bend, taking the long way to get back to his dorm as it would avoid having to walk alongside the others. His dorm was across campus, some five minutes to walk on a good day. Maybe a ten-minute stumble. He wandered back home, flicking on the light, and nearly vomited again as the lights pierced his cloudy eyes. His feet shuffled through the room, a messy amalgamation of unkempt fortitude.

Clothes were strewn around as if launched from a cannon, lacking any rhyme or reason as they cloaked stains that formed crop circles in the carpet. A bottle of some half empty liquor clanged around a bit as he stepped over it, carefully stepping into piles of mess like he was avoiding landmines.

He kicked a little, feebly attempting some sort of maneuver, and when it didn't work, he didn't even bother kicking off his shoes, nor taking off his jacket, as his legs floundered towards his bed like a newly born faun. He didn't know if it was the alcohol or the drugs, but the world around him sloshed violently, the kind of seasickness he experienced from a usual blackout, but his mind persisted, lingering in the same dim corners as his vision. He plopped down, face first, letting the warmth of the bed coddle him as the fuzzy blankets bordered on overstimulating to the touch. He waited for the room to stop spinning before drifting off to a welcomed sleep.

HE AWOKE TO A full call history, scrolling through the multiple messages left when his finger froze, his eyes not believing what he was seeing. Two missed calls from Emily rested below his finger, with a corresponding voice mail in his inbox.

He held the phone up to his ear and began to listen. Her voice was frantic, angered. "Stop trying to contact me. First you show up at my house, out of the blue, just appear back in my life. You're the one that said you couldn't be friends, Adam, not me. Then you use Thomas, our friend's, attempted suicide as...what? A way to talk to me at the bar? A fucking conversation starter? I was worried about you. I was truly worried about you and then you pull this shit? You drunk call me in the middle of the night saying how I'm gonna die because you saw it in some drug fueled dream? I'm not gonna hang myself, but I am gonna get the cops involved if you dare fucking call me again. You need help, Adam, whatever you took that night. You had a nightmare. But you need to deal with the fact that we've been separated for longer than we were together, and I know that scares you, but you can't call someone saying you foresaw them killing themselves and turning your own friends attempted suicide into...what? A way for you to martyr your way back into my pants? One day, sooner or later, you'll have to accept that things ended the way they did for a reason."

Her voice trailed off as a round of knocking permeated through the speaker, rapid and frantic. "And who the fuck keeps doing that? I swear to God if that's you at my door, Adam..." A clambering erupted through the phone like she had stood and begun walking to the door, where the knocking intensified, growing increasingly sporadic as it fell off any discernible rhythm. The creaking of a door opening filled the air, then a simple, guttural, "Holy shit," before the line went dead.

Atari flashed through his phone, past multiple outgoing messages he must've left Emily the night before, and found one more voice mail. He flicked his finger onto it, shuffling the little icon so that it began to play. Gal's elusive voice sprung up, monotonically spraying, "Atari, me and Cass are down by the east wing dorms. You need to come. Now."

Atari looked; the message was only seventeen minutes old. He found new purpose, overcoming his hangover in mere seconds, leaping out of bed, still wearing the clothes from last night, he took off for the door. East wing was where Emily's dorm was located and that, mixed with the cryptic ending of her phone call, didn't bode well. The dorms spread across most of the campus, interlacing with one another at certain points, and he knew he'd have to make some shortcuts, racing between bushes and through crowds of people that didn't seem to know the urgency of the situation just a few minutes' walk away.

ATARI RAN PAST THE lawn at the center of campus. Past the pond. Past the cautionary tape that spider-webbed her dorm's hall until an officer stopped him, muscular, outstretched arms keeping him at bay. "No civilians past the line," he growled, though Atari's brain ignored the details of the man's face.

Atari, driven by the vision of Emily's body swaying from the rafters, duck-and-weaved the cop, trying to find an opening to get past him. He saw a glimpse of her door from over his shoulder and was terrified to see a thick stream of blood drug down its frame, bloodied handprints centipeding either side.

The blood oozed down the door, coagulating into a puddle on the floor that reminded him of the one Trigger had been found in. "I need to get through. You don't understand! I know the person that lives there and—"

"Adam?"

He paused, stunned by the voice, and turned to see Cass coddling Emily on a nearby bench. Atari watched as Cass rubbed her fingertips down Emily's arm, an almost longing in the embrace that he felt himself grow unjustly jealous of. How long had it been since he had touched her like that? Held her like that?

"Adam?" Emily called out again, her voice meek.

Atari rushed over to her, so much excitement flooding his chest that he had to fight off the urge to wrap her in an embrace when he got to her. She was alive. Startled. Shaken. But alive. "Em? I thought you were—"

She lunged, burying herself in his chest and gripping his shirt with an iron grasp. "It was horrible, Adam. Just horrible."

Atari's face turned. "What? What happened?"

"Sabrina...she...she...I just don't know what got into her. There was this knocking, and I thought it was- I just thought someone was at the door. But then I went to open it and it was just so horrible, Adam. She was slamming her face against it. Just one time after another, leaving imprints in its frame. I couldn't get her to stop. She just kept pounding, over and over. Her teeth were already missing by the time I opened it. Her eye...her one eye just popped. It just fucking popped. By the time I got her to stop, there was so little left. It wasn't real. It couldn't be real. It wasn't human."

Her tears began seeping through Atari's shirt, soaking his chest as she clutched him, wobbling slightly. He reached down, awkwardly patting her head as she muttered aimlessly, any semblance of coherency to her words lost in his chest.

Then he had a thought. "Em, is there any chance that Sabrina had started taking any pills? Anything new? Something that she'd have any reason to hide?"

Emily pulled away slightly, her one hand reaching back to rummage through her purse. She pulled out a baggy of those iridescent, chalky, almost hazy pills that matched the ones Atari and Trigger had taken. "Like these?" she whimpered. "Sabrina got real paranoid yesterday. She made me hold on to them. I just— I just thought they were like weed pills...I don't know. I don't do that stuff. Why, what is it?"

"We don't know," Cass said, casually pushing the baggy into her shoe as a cop wandered by, "but it's the exact same shit that Trigger took."

"Before he—?"

"Yeah. Before he did that."

10

— . —

THE PLUG

CASS, EMILY, AND ATARI made their way back to Gal, who in turn drove them to Butch and Annabelle's place. The small gang recounted their story, Emily able to talk with a bit more clarity but still cycling into sobs with every other sentence.

When everyone had finished Atari slammed the baggy of pills onto the table, boldly announcing, "These pills. They're the catalyst for everything. Me and Trigger took them, then Sabrina took them. We just have to figure out what they are and where they got them from. Anyone have any ideas?"

Cass raised her hand tentatively, as if she wasn't sure she should. "I know Trigger's main dealer...she's right here on campus. Ethel something, third year biology student."

"That's a great place to start," Atari stated, attempting to pump some optimism into his voice. "So, we go and we find her, come on everyone—"

"No, no, Atari," Cass deflected, "if a whole squadron pulls up to her dorm, she's gonna get squirmy and not tell us anything. This has to be a small group mission, maybe just two of us. And one should be me. I know Ethel. I've bought from her before. She'll be more likely to talk if I'm around."

"Then it's settled. Em?"

Emily's hand had shot up in the air, her eyes still peering at some invisible spot on the ground. Atari noticed her other hand rested on Annabelle's lap, their pinkies entangled. "But Sabrina never bought from Ethel. They had a thing...Ethel got with her ex, so she refused to talk to her. I think Sabrina's dealer's name was Brad."

Annabelle piped in, "Me and Gal will go see Brad then. See if we can get any information out of him while you two go after Ethel. One of them is bound to know something. Butchy can stay behind and watch over Emily in case she needs anything."

Butch silently nodded along as Emily's eyes flickered up to meet him for a fraction of a second, as if testing if he'd be a suitable caretaker. Atari felt it, that great, unnatural sense of jealousy fluttering throughout his chest, just watching Emily put her trust in someone else. He swallowed it, sensing how irrational it was before turning back to the others.

"Alright, sounds like it's settled. We split up, cover more ground, Scooby-Doo style, and then hunt down the source of the pills."

The group agreed, forming into the right clusters and taking off toward their cars. Atari shot one last look at Emily as she stifled a sob. He could've sworn for just a second her gaze rose to match him before he spun around, led out the door by Cass. They piled into Atari's car, taking off into the blinding light of day.

CASS LED THE WAY down the endless expanse of twisting monotony that made up the dorm rooms with familiarity. Her eyes tracked the names on the doors, searching for Ethel's name to pop up. "It's around here somewhere," she told Atari, who had never been in this building before.

She pounded down a set of stairs, making a harsh right, and found herself right in front of the door branded with that elusive name. "Here's the one." She cried, a bit too excitedly, and had to cull her desperation for answers. Did she even believe what was happening? This talk of demons, of some sort of evil, Lovecraftian spirit. It made no sense and yet her one friend was in the hospital with two others making the same claims. She knew she had to do something to get answers, to figure out what had happened to spiral their lives so harshly into the abstract.

She bravely knocked on the door, eyes flickering towards Atari, who bounced awkwardly on his toes, not masking his own desperation very well. They were all friends, sure, but it had always been Atari and Trigger, first and foremost. The two were inseparable after Emily and Atari's breakup, going on prolonged binges and road trips on a whim, while the others struggled to keep up with their impulsiveness.

Cass's thoughts were cut off as the door creaked open a bit. "David?" a voice hissed through the crack.

"Not David, it's me, Cass."

"Cass?" The door slammed shut. There was the clinking of a lock, and then it opened again, wider this time. Ethel was short, with dyed white hair that juxtaposed dark brown eyebrows and thick pouting lips that quivered a little with each step she took. A stout arm beckoned them into the room and the door was slammed shut behind them.

"You run out already, Cass?" Ethel questioned. "That normally lasts you a month, doesn't it? Might be time for a tolerance break." As she talked, she crawled under a table, unscrewing the bolts on a vent pressed against the wall.

"It's not us, Ethel, it's Trigger—"

"Thomas knows he can come himself, doesn't he? The boy has legs, last I checked, and they worked as they should—"

"He's in the—"

"—act of doing something...right now." Cass hastily cut off Atari, shooting him a 'let me do the talking,' kind of glance. "You know, Trigger, he gets paranoid sometimes, so he sent us to pick some stuff up for him."

Ethel seemed to accept that answer, swiveling back to unscrewing the vent. "Alright, so what can I do ya for this time? Can't do any L right now. David's picking up my last supplies here in a few."

"That's ok, we need...something else."

"Well? Out with it."

"Well, we don't exactly know the name. It's new, something he hadn't had before. Some pills, kinda a...weird color—"

"Kronos." Atari shot out, and both figures turned to stare at him. "He called it Kronos. Do you have anything that goes by that name?" Ethel shot him a quizzical look, her body retracting, and he immediately knew he had said something wrong.

"I already told your friend that was the last of the Kronos I had or would be getting. Stuff's practically impossible to get your hands on, it's barely even hit the streets yet, like I told him, I was just unloading the stock I had leftover."

"Then how'd you get your hands on it?" Cass asked, eyes going wide as she immediately knew she had fucked up as well.

"One thing about dealing, you never tell where you get your supplies from. Best-case scenario, the buyer cuts out the middleman and worst case they piss off upper management and lose you a supplier. These people, they're like any man, they like tight lips. You should know this by now, Cassandra."

"I know but—"

"There is no but. Shop's closed, I'm gonna have to ask you to leave." She began gesturing towards the door, trying to shepherd them out of it. "I don't know what you're trying to get out of all these questions, but I really just can't help you."

"Ethel—"

"No!"

The door unlatched. Atari was growing desperate. "Ethel, please, Trigger is in the hospital."

Ethel paused for a second, a look of pain stretching across her face before she opened the door. "All the more reason to kick you out, unfortunately. I can't be tied to that. Everything I give is of good quality. What people tend to do with it is out of my control."

"Ethel, please," Cass began as she was ushered out of the room.

"No, I'm sorry but—"

"I took the pills," Atari exploded. "I took them and I'm seeing things now and I don't know what's real or not real and I'm scared, and we need your help. Whatever happened to Trigger, whatever's gonna happen to me, we gotta know how to stop it. You've gotta know something."

"It's hallucinogenic, you're going to see things..." Ethel stated, seemingly unsure of herself.

"Not this...not something like this. This is real. Tangible."

Ethel perused the room, making a big effort in avoiding contact with Atari's eyes. Cass watched, surprised at Atari for standing his ground, and respected the fortitude in his unnaturally defiant stance.

"Hanson...Hamilton Hanson. Doubt it's his real name, but it's a start. He's where I got the pills from, but the problem is, I've never actually met him. He drops. I pick up and deliver. That's our deal. I don't know much about Kronos besides that it was in the last drop and had a little note attached to it with a phrase and a price."

"What phrase?" Cass pondered.

"Delve into the future by seeking out the past. I don't know, just some bullshit hippy-speak that these kinds of people like to throw around. Now, just don't go willy-nilly costing me clients, alright? Keep it on the hush...and I wish the best for your friend. Thomas is a good one." The door slammed behind them.

Atari looked over at Cass. "Well- we have a name."

"We have a moniker, but it's a start."

They began their trek back through the twisted labyrinth of dorm rooms and communal spaces, endlessly lapping the same monotony as they swam their way back to the main entrance. Cass watched Atari gain a few steps on her, his confidence pulsating through each step as his steps began to grow rapid, hungry to find more information.

He loved her; she thought. He really loved her, and he'd do anything to protect her. To safeguard Emily, he'd walk through fire. The thought of which made Cass' stomach churn and brought with it a slew of painful memories that had regressed into the corners of her mind that now recovered the light. What she had done...if he ever found out. She shook her head, trying to rid herself of the thoughts, when she noticed he had gone a full dozen paces ahead of her in his mad rush. She watched as he went through the doors to the outside, then watched in horror as those same doors slammed on their own with an alien might.

She ran over, attempting to pry the handle open, but it was locked. More than locked. The door didn't budge at all, almost as if she was tugging on the wall. The usual permeating scuttle of breeze that would lap its way through cracks was entirely absent. Cass spun and was hit by an almost immediate sense of vertigo, the room swinging as if she was aboard a ship and the lights dimmed out of existence, leaving her to peer through a darkened hellscape that abandoned all rational ideology as the outside daylight failed to flutter into the catacombs.

She screamed, and not a sound came out, as if the air sponged her voice away. She knew she needed to find help, so she rushed over to the closest room, knocking on the great wooden door and attempted to pry that open, too, to no avail. The room spun worse now, whirling around her with the same illusionary distortion as a funhouse. She spun, near vomiting, as her heart escaped through each pore of her sweat soaked body. She attempted to enter each door, and with each attempt came the realization that the doors themselves were like wallpaper fixtures that merely mocked the essence of their perceived device, like a looney-tunes style painting of a tunnel that she fell for every time.

She scrambled, trying the fourth door when a scurrying sound caught her ear. The disgusting scuttle of a thousand legs added to the surreal wackiness as they sounded like a Scooby-Doo character running with all their might, charging for her as she pushed her way further down into nothingness. She ran, driven by an all-encompassing fear, when she pushed through a door that, to her surprise, actually opened, leading her straight to a staircase. Shadows closed in on either side of the staircase from where it rose to where it dropped, only allowing her a few feet of sight yet she was able to see the pair of legs that stuck out a few steps up, the body blending into a sharp abstract.

Cass called out to the person, bleating, "Help! Help me, please!" She stumbled up a few steps, arm extended to grasp the legs, but withdrew as sight found horror. She watched as the legs exploded into a geyser of other limbs where a torso would sit. A jumble of replicated legs that twitched and spasmed in the open air. The beast's initial legs bent backwards, muscles curving around the bones like the joints didn't exist. The creature somersaulted down a few steps, landing on a few of the other legs that expounded from its base. Cass squealed, petrified from the horror as she watched the cluster of legs scuttle closer, and it was within this horror that she realized that was the beast's entire makeup. Just legs interspersed by a porous array of vacuous vaginal openings, the labia peeled back to expose the inner workings of a tubal pulsating muscular cluster.

Cass was stricken by a strange wave of recollection, her eyes shifting between the blurs of movement, switching between the twitching legs and running down the bushy curls of hair that surrounded each fold of flesh. She knew, somehow, impossibly knew that what she was seeing had been ripped straight from Emily's body, as if an exact replica of her exposed legs, each birthmark or scar placed exactly how it should be.

She pivoted, ready to race down the stairs when her clumsy legs snagged the shadows, sending her spiraling down them. She felt something snap. An immediate, overwhelming pressure began building up in her leg. She tried to stand, and the pain nearly sent her into convulsions. The creature pounced, bounding effortlessly down the stairs and landing on top of Cass, who fought to crawl away. She felt it lay on her, a wetness dripping onto her skin as its weight began to bore into her chest.

She screamed, failing lungs caught between desperate attempts at inhaling. Her eyes blackened, the circular vision she had already been encapsulated in shrinking even further as the pressure consumed her every waking thought, the beast melding with her flesh as caustic burns sprouted anywhere it touched.

She went through stages. Quickly, each one flashing by in an instant. Horror. Disgust. Perseverance.

Melancholy. Acceptance. All accumulating in an almost allure-like quality to her death, savoring the moments before the last of the air had been vanquished, when the door flung open, exploding light into the dank abyss. The second the light touched the being it was gone, the weight lifted as if it had never even existed and Cass pulled as much oxygen into her depleted lungs as she could, gargling on the sickening sweetness of the air.

Her mind flickered back to Emily, her naked body bent over a pillow, ass plunged towards the sky while she rested on her arms and knees. Cass's hands fumbled to caress Em's body, desperately trying to hide the shaking of each appendage as she sloshed around drunkenly. She knew, even in the moment, she knew what she was doing. How badly it would hurt Atari if he ever found out. Still, she gave over her body to the year of pent-up lust.

She groped Emily's ass and her heart fluttered, watching the way the fat gave to her grip, spilling out around her fingers with a surprising thickness for how skinny Emily was. Emily moaned, Cass followed, mimicking each other's cries as she took her tongue to Emily's skin, running it down lightning bolt like a web of stretch marks. Emily quivered.

Cass continued her onslaught, tongue pressed until she was wrapping it around Emily's labia, circling it like a finger on a topological map.

Atari. All she could think about the entire time was Atari. Even as she entered Emily. Even under the ecstasy of Emily's squeals. Even after getting what she had always wanted.

Her eyes recoiled in her skull, blasting her back to reality.

She heard Atari before she saw him, her eyes briefly taking in his boots running towards her as she curled into a ball, still heaving. Cass could feel him dive beside her, wrapping her in an embrace from behind as she wailed a screaming sob into her chest, body rocking with such an intense force that she couldn't begin to control it.

Arms clung to her body anywhere they could reach. His. Hers. She couldn't so much as tell the difference, nor did she care. She just wanted to be wrapped in their comforting warmness. His breath was hot on her neck. She tried to balance herself with that, syncing his breathing to her own as she felt their chests give and push simultaneously. "Atari, Atari, please...please." She whimpered, feeling like a kid calling for their mother, though the embarrassment was outweighed by the horrific trauma placed upon her.

"What is it?" he puffed, his voice making a desperate attempt to sound soothing despite the fact that he too was bleating to fill his lungs. "I turned around, and you were just gone...just like that. What is it? What did you see?"

How was she supposed to tell him? How was she supposed to accept his comforting grasp after what she had done to him...done with Emily? Still, despite guilt welling up inside her like the flames of a hot stove, greed won over. She found her arms accepting his embrace, molding her body around it as she gripped his hands, leading them around her waist. "I can't...I can't...I can't-"

"It's ok," he soothed, obviously getting the message and pivoting, "You don't have to say anything, it's gonna be ok. Remember- remember in grade school. Remember our art project, in Miss. Keilings class. We had to paint the Mona Lisa, remember? And I- I just couldn't. I was never very good at drawing, and I was terrified that the drawings were gonna be hung up on the wall for everyone to see. I went through so many shitty stick figures, so many rough attempts at drawing something- anything of intrinsic value. Anything I could proudly display. And when the time came to turn it in, I hated mine so much that I came to school early and ripped it off the wall. Threw it in the trash and covered it up."

He laughed to himself, a forced laugh, but one Cass found a sense of comfort in. "You must've been watching me do it. We didn't even really know each other back then, just in passing, but you must've dug through the trash for mine. You hung it up right in the middle of the displays, right next to yours. A gaudy, monstrous depiction of the Mona Lisa, something that would make Da Vinci roll in his grave. Yours had- what?"

"A snake—" Cass whimpered.

"Yeah, a snake wrapped around her throat. Biting her eyeball out. She was screaming and had this panic-stricken look on her face and the entire thing was such a mess you could hardly tell if it was a snake or a lump of shit with fangs, but you didn't care. You were so brave. So controlling of the room that I envied you. I do...envy you."

"I just—"

"I never did get the chance to thank you for that. Without that, I would've never had the guts to enter that talent show, or that poetry competition. I would've never been able to get up from falling on my face without you, Cass, you know that?"

Cass' breathing began to slow, their heart rate sinking into the folds of Atari's voice as he continued. "I never would've gotten my diagnosis without you, either. Remember. I was too scared to even enter a therapist's room, let alone confront myself. My BPD, the sides of me I couldn't face. You knew all along; you followed me through the worst of it and you're the reason I came out the other side. You and Annabelle, and...and," his voice trailed off before dropping the last word, though Cass knew he was choking on the name, "Trigger."

"Atari..." Her senses had begun to return to her. Feeling the chilled breath of the stone floor. The stale air of the unventilated hall. Atari's shaking legs pressed into the back of hers.

"You know what I'm gonna do when I graduate?

"No—"

"Neither do I," he sighed, almost enthusiastically. "I don't have a goddamn clue what I'm meant to do in this world. I'm not a great artist. I'm not a leader. I'm not someone that leaves that kind of a mark. My hands will always just be hands. I used to resent them for that. I used to take my pen, and I'd- I'd stab into them when nobody was around. When they refused to create something beautiful. I used to wish the world was ending so I wouldn't have to choose whether to end it myself. But I'll always have you, and that makes me special."

She was okay. She had to remind herself that she was okay as she melted into Atari's arms, allowing his grip to console her. He was strong. Much stronger than she had ever anticipated him to be, his elongated tangle of limbs flexing instinctively as they physically and emotionally planted her to the ground.

Had she ever been held in such an embrace? Hugged, yes. Much more than that, even, but never with this level of love. Never with such a fiery passion.

Cass thought carefully for a second, running her tongue along the seat of her teeth as if testing if they'd bite it off before she spoke. "You know I used to wish I was dying just so I could have a reason to actually live. I was so terrified of not being extraordinary that I was consumed by this overwhelming lust to just be ordinary. I figured if life couldn't make me great, the least it could do was make me belong. I always struggled with that...belonging. Finding a place that would actually accept me. The boys didn't want the girl around. The girls didn't want the lesbian. You know kids, they're cruel. Then I found you guys and- and I'm sorry Atari- though she couldn't bring herself to say what for.

"It's nothing, trust me- whatever you think it is...it's nothing."

Cass pivoted her body around, rotating in his arms until she was facing him. He was sobbing, tears trickling down his cheeks in expansive pools that probably mirrored her own. She began grounding herself with her surroundings.

Something she could feel. Atari. His firm yet gentle grasp, the way his soft chest basically enveloped her face.

Something she could hear. Her own breathing. Manic. She had to slow her breathing to loosen up her chest.

Something she could smell. Shampoo. Atari's shampoo smelled like freshly picked strawberries.

She ran through every sense, over and over, until her breathing began to crawl, only spiking every so often when a jagged sob returned. Then, suddenly, realization came over her. "We gotta leave," she croaked, gently pushing his body away so she could prop herself up. "Now!"

"What's wrong? We're alright, okay?"

"You and Trigger both took the pills, right? That's why we thought you could see it. Why we thought it could affect you. But I just saw it, hell it damn near killed me. Atari. If I can see it, if it can attack me, then how do we know the others are safe?"

Atari's eyes bounced around as if reading his thoughts on the air, "Yeah...yeah no, we need to leave."

11

BLOSSOMING

PAST

"EMILY...EMILY, I THINK THIS is our stop." The bus lurched to a stop; its innards ravaged by a desperate mob that pushed their way out before the wheels had even stopped spinning. Atari stood, taking Emily's hand and following Cass and Trigger from the carnage. Gal waddled behind them, all of them taking to the city sidewalk where an even larger crowd pushed past for onboarding.

Atari's head spun around, taking in the majestic jungle of wealthy monoliths crashing around an open sky. Hollywood. Thousands of buildings swarmed the skyline, marking an almost Lovecraftian grandeur as Atari found himself feeling so small he could hardly stand it. He took out his phone, snapping various pictures of his surroundings. Far from a professional photographer, but the pretty cityscape yielded good results, regardless.

"We finally did it. We're actually here guys! Isn't it beautiful?" Atari cooed, cars creaked by and for the first time in a while, the thought to turn into the street didn't cross his mind. "Even at night, it feels so lively. This is a place where I could see myself really living."

"You know someone took your wallet a few blocks back, right?" Trigger snarked as he waddled ahead of the pack, doing a little shimmy as he checked to make sure his own wallet was still in his pocket.

"Yeah, but he looked scary, and I only had a twenty on me, anyway."

"You drove halfway across the country on a twenty?" Annabelle judged.

Atari shrugged. "You wouldn't let me stop at a bank, and that's all I had in my room. Although now buying a drink is gonna need some bartering."

Emily danced into view, brandishing a twisted grin. "I'll go and buy you one, milady."

"And what's the catch?"

"No, catch, just kindness," she pranced off, arms tethered behind her back as she scoped her surroundings. When she settled on a stand, she whisked two sodas from a freezer and waltzed up to a counter that proudly displayed a vast collage of collectables, anything from souvenirs to trinkets of various sizes, more like leftover scraps from a yard sale than a storefront. Her malicious eyes bobbed up and down the row until she pointed at something on the back shelf, the clerk turning his attention towards it as they made small talk. Em had obviously asked to see the item as the clerk pulled out a miniature ladder, crawling up its rungs.

Em's eyes flickered to one of the guards as she held a decorative cat that she had been surveying from the counter, then bouncing to the clerk, then the guards, then to her friends, and in a split second she was barreling down the crowd towards them, her expansive hair bouncing with each elongated stride. Atari got a quick glance at the guard's pursuit before being yanked around by the arm as Emily led him down the spiraling neon streets. The crowd swallowed the others as Atari watched the bobbing brown streak that flowed before him. His breath was too sharp to speak, and his mind too flooded with adrenaline to process as he followed.

They spun past a hotdog vender as its owner croaked Russian, past the reflection of gilded stars, pocketing dense shadows where they danced upon the universe, and down muddied alleyways which harshly contrasted the irradiated grandeur of the neon gods. They ran for what seemed like miles until they collapsed onto a bench at an outdoor food vendor near a park that marked a small pocket away from the clutter.

"I could've...lent you...some...some money...for the dumb plastic cat," Atari gasped as he sputtered for oxygen, his entire body heaving. He remembered why he didn't run. Why, he had never run. The unpleasant pain that bubbled in his chest almost too much to bear.

She plopped it down, admiring its fluorescent colors as she wheezed, "I think it's glass..."

"Oh, yeah...that makes a big difference......I...I'm strictly against buying glass," he sighed, his head bobbing against the table as the flames in his chest began to die down.

"I don't know. I just kinda wanted it. I didn't steal it, I mean not really...I slipped a hundred into his pocket when his back was turned. The cat only cost seventy-five, so I made it worth the trouble."

"Then why take it?"

She shrugged as she spun the cat and started to inspect the other side. "Have you ever been chased by security before?"

"Of course not."

She beamed at him. "Neither had I, but now I have. Exhilarating, wasn't it? We gotta start living Golden Boy, like really living. The whole, surrender yourself to your inhibitions. Yes, man type experience, ya know. Knock a few things off the bucket list."

Atari clutched his pounding chest. The blood was still rocking through his body, expelled through the pounding of his ears and throat as he found himself mirroring the smile that encapsulated her face. "But how did you-"

"Remember when we watched 'A Place Further Than the Universe' together? Ever since that day I've been imagining being chased through a big city with you and I wanted to before I couldn't—" her voice fed into the silence of the barren streets atmosphere.

"What do you—?"

"The moon is beautiful, isn't it?" He followed her gaze to the crystalline cyclops. When he didn't respond she gazed intently into his eyes, "You know Soseki Natsumi said that the best way to translate the English phrase 'I love you' into Japanese was 'the moon is beautiful, isn't it' I think about that a lot. Whenever I'm looking at the moon, I want to call you, but then I start to think maybe it's been too long, maybe he doesn't want us anymore, maybe he'll become some big success and leave behind his failure friends. You've always been so impressive, Atari. So talented, so...I don't know, driven? Whatever it is, you've always had it and I just keep thinking what if we graduate and I never tell him-"

"Emily?"

"Maybe that's all true, but I've realized I might have to act soon if I'm going to." Her eyes floated back to the moon. Atari shifted to take up the gap between them, pressing his body into the static of open air.

To his surprise, she bent in, waltzing through the space between them and placing her lips lightly onto his, as if allowing him the space to pull away. When he didn't, she pressed a little harder, and further to his surprise, he reciprocated, feeling the warmth of her pillowy lips. Her lips immediately felt like a home he had never had. Like each concave, each little atom was made specifically to fit with his, to interlock in such a way that made them almost impossible to pull apart. Their first kiss. Their first perfect moment.

12

POSSESSION

PRESENT

"THEY SHOULD'VE BEEN BACK hours ago," Emily whimpered to nobody in particular.

"Maybe their mission was a bit more lucrative than ours?" Annabelle pondered, her eyes bouncing between Butch and Emily.

"Yeah...maybe." Still, Emily's eyes never left the window, longingly peering out into the driveway. Two cars sat out front, neither of which were Atari's. "Something just feels off...this whole situation, I mean the things Adam mentioned seeing they're...absurd, right?" Now it was Annabelle's turn to shrug, "You're the one that said you saw what you saw. And I really don't think that's much crazier than what he's been saying."

"Yeah..."

Emily's eyes withdrew from the sheen of glass, head turning to face the others, and caught a flash of movement out the corner of her eye. She looked back, and it was gone. Just like that, just gone.

She opened her mouth to speak, interrupted by the room exploding into chaos as the shattering of glass erupted from an adjacent room. Her eyes immediately took her back to that scene. Back to the door, with her roommate bashing her concave skull against the door frame, the dull, meaty thuds echoing, penetrating her ears. She saw it all in a brilliant flash, each detail perfectly encapsulated. The way the fluid in her eyes peeled off the wall, like cum off the tongue, dribbling onto the blood-soaked ground.

The way her nose smashed against her face as if all the bones had been flattened, crinkling against each other with the repetitive smashing motion. The way her hair clung to portions of exposed bone that prodded in a placid jumble of white on red, hidden underneath a casing of blue bruises like her entire face was mocking the American flag's scheme.

She flashed back to reality just as jarringly, her knees buckling under her so dramatically that Butch had to flounder his arms around her to keep from collapsing. They all looked at Emily, but she nodded before they could speak. "Gal?" she wailed, commenting on the room's only missing occupant.

Butch shook his head, "Bathroom still. Said he was getting a nosebleed."

"Pretty bad one too," Annabelle said. "It just kept gushing blood."

Butch led the way into the living room, Emily grappling for a large cooking knife as they entered the room where cool air forced its way through the spiraling of cracks of a destroyed window frame, chunks of snowflake-like glass scattered around the room.

Butch knelt down, gingerly grasping a larger piece and holding it up to the frame like he was examining a puzzle piece, his face contorting. "It's not cold enough to bust a window like that. And there's nothing around here that could've shattered it..." Their eyes followed the creaking of wood to Gal, who had just entered the room, a bloodied flag of white cropping from his nose like he was surrendering. His eyes glinted with something that threw Emily off, a sort of malice that she had never seen in his face before.

Emily gazed out the window and felt her organs shift in her stomach as a looming figure stared within the small house, its featureless face pivoted as though looking directly at her despite not having any eyes to stare from. It stood, some fifteen feet tall, on an elongated humanoid body like someone had steamrolled an NBA player. It didn't move, nor did it seem capable of doing so, planting into the ground like a mirage more so than an actual being. She stared as it stood there in unmoving awe, her knees nearly giving way as the being's head shifted ever so slightly, as if gesturing towards where Gal stood behind her.

Butch cleared his throat to say something, pulling Emily from her trance, when another window burst just as effortlessly, pieces scattering across the room like a heavy wind had taken them hostage. Then another. Then another. Every window in the house combusting one after the other, leading to a trail of amalgamated sound. Emily screamed, unable to contain her lungs as glass sprayed the air in massive bursts, caking up dust and debris. Each pop intermixed with the residual memory of her friend's head bursting at the seams.

Then, the house ran out of windows as all sound died out. Butch stayed squatting for a few moments, shielding his face, and only stood again once they were all sure that the crashing had ceased. "Well, that was certainly—"

A little whimper came from Emily's right, leading to an explosive shout just as shattering and overwhelming as the broken glass. She looked over just as Gal doubled over, latching onto his stomach in a taut grip as he squealed into himself. His back squared, spine prodding at the skin as if some great boney snake was attempting to pierce from a cocoon, stabbing through layers of muscle. He shook, an otherworldly belch of pain springing caustically from his lungs. Every vein in his throat expanded, flaring up like the frill of a lizard.

Emily was the first to react, reaching for him from behind. Her hand bent close, ready to squeeze his shoulder when his body shot backwards, back overextending to such a point that Emily could hear the bones splinter as they shot through his chest and throat, yanking at the sinews of skin that clung on. He screamed. Screamed until no other sound could be heard as his back bent further, then further still, an impossible sort of bend that defied the body's capabilities more than any acrobat. His ribs pushed through the skin, tearing the body to shreds and a broken neck lulled behind him, the back of his head making contact with the square of his back in such a way that would've killed any man. Still, he screamed. Bellowed. Chanted in a foreign tongue.

Emily stumbled backwards, colliding with the wall, and his screaming ceased at the sound, morphing into a clattering of teeth as they violently gnashed within his skull. He lunged, body still flipped backwards, his arms clawing for her when she raised hers in defense. Em hit the wall, sandwiched between it and Gal in a flash. Gal's eyes widening and a warm sensation spreading throughout her torso, almost as if she had pissed herself. No, she thought, not piss...blood.

She looked down; she was still holding the knife, the hilt of which permeated out of Gal's gut, blood expanding from the wound and onto her body. Her mind buzzed, consuming input on a delay as if everything was muffled through a drug addled veil, her friends screaming various phrases that incoherently bounced off her ears. She looked into the rapidly emptying eyes of her friend and squeezed her eyes shut, hoping the world would just end right there.

When it didn't, when the screaming continued, she opened her eyes. Gal stood there, right in the middle of the room, feet away from where he had been moments ago. His back had straightened to its regular position, no evidence of it ever bending in the first place besides the black hilt of a blood-soaked knife that perforated out his back like a single hedgehog quill.

His wails were drowned out by the cries of the others as the room broke into madness. "Holy fuck, holy fucking fuck!" Annabelle yelped, backing up until her ass collided with a table. "You fucking stabbed him."

"No...no, it's not what it looks like," Emily spat. She motioned to raise her hands submissively, only noticing she was still holding the blade when she accidentally pried it from the man's back and let it clatter to the floor. Gal squealed, an unearthly squawk as he fumbled to reach for his blood soaked back, tugging on the shirt and spinning around to look into Emily's eyes.

"Em-Emily?" he whimpered, confusion and fear consuming his words as recollection spread across his face, eyes dropping to the knife on the ground, then raising back up to Emily's one last time before his body dropped to join it. The rag dolled body immediately transformed into a corpse in her mind. Not her friend. Not Gal. Just that, some corpse. She stepped backwards, putting some space between her and the body and went to call out to her friends, "Wait. Guys, just...just wait."

Annabelle slipped on the coagulating pool of blood as she dove towards the body, overcoming her shock as she frantically fumbled for a pulse.

Nothing. Before she even spoke, Emily could tell by her face that she found nothing. Her head whipped towards Emily, "You...you fucking killed him!"

"No, I- I- I—"

"Call an ambulance. Butch! Call an ambulance!"

Butch's body reclaimed life, snapping into movement and attempting to drag Annabelle away from the body as her limbs thrashed around. His eyes never left Emily. "We gotta move. We can't stay here, we gotta move. Now!"

"She fucking stabbed him!"

"I didn't! I— he came after me! His spine broke when he bent backwards and then he came after me!" Emily squealed, attempting to strip the blood from her shirt with her fingernails, snapping one off in the process. "I swear, I didn't- I wouldn't."

"He was just standing there! Just- just standing there when you—"

"No, he came after me."

Butch had Annabelle by the pits, dragging her away when they both tripped over something. All three's eyes flickered to the knife.

"Anna...Anna calm down-" Emily pleaded, whipping out a shivering hand like she was trying to sooth a dog, blood raining off her skin where it was lapped up by a greedy carpet.

Annabelle flung her body towards the knife, scooping it up and brandishing it towards Emily like a spear. "I'll fucking kill you, you bitch!" Her body tensed, poised to strike, Emily raising her arms defensively, when the room shifted once more.

A great clattering of bones meshing at inhuman angles shot through the air like poppers as Gal's body rose as if puppeteered, hovering like a magician's act. It clung to lifeless-ness, head lulling lackadaisically. For a few seconds of abstract horror, it simply hovered there, Emily completely unsure if what she was seeing was even reality anymore as all three stared at the levitating corpse. Then the blood that outlined the corpse on the floor began to shift, separating itself from the carpet and stretching through the air like a liquid hand where it groped for the corpse, slithering up its leg and re-entering the wound where it had just escaped.

The wound filled itself back up; the blood sealing itself away within the corpse as if it had never spilled in the first place. It wasn't until the last drop had been reclaimed by its host that the body was overtaken by a sputtering wave of nauseating spasms.

Butch, Annabelle, and Emily all watched as the corpse jerked back to life, legs planting themselves on the ground, and something adjacent to sentience emerging from between the piercing veins of his eyes. It stood there, not in Gal's typical stance, nor anything human, but standing as if it were a marionette, its face still slack.

"G-Gal?" Annabelle whispered. Then, a little louder, "Gal?"

Gal's body was thrusted forward, yanked into place by invisible hands as it stumbled a step, then another, gaining speed with each step as it flung itself at Annabelle. She weaved, dodging just in time, and the corpse of their friend splattered the table, sending it spiraling as the force of his body lacked any sense of self preservation. Annabelle spun, eyes following the rag dolled corpse as it rose already, less standing, more drug to its feet as its bones popped out at awkward angles.

Annabelle spun to run when she tripped, tumbling to the ground and the corpse of Gal was on top of her before she had the chance to scream, clawing at her with its ravenous limbs. It tore with an impossible strength, making quick work of both clothes and flesh with each slash. Emily screamed, backing herself against the wall. Butch somersaulted towards the entangled bodies, a demented beast with two backs. The linebacker tackled the corpse of Gal. Both bodies hit the floor, tumbling a bit.

Emily dashed forward, scooping Annabelle off the ground, while Butch struggled to keep the corpse from rising once more. They ran, making it to the end of the room, when Annabelle stopped. "Butch?"

Butch stood in the middle of the room, panting hard as the sound of his name caught his ear. "Run!" he shouted just as he rocketed off his feet.

They spun, making a mad dash down the hall and towards the bedroom, immediately barricading the door with a nearby dresser. They huddled as far against the wall as they could, Annabelle wrapping her arms around Emily as she shuddered through her fear. The sounds of struggling continued, two bodies bashing against each other like rams, as one after the other was flung against the floor and walls. Emily struggled to adjust her ringing ears enough to make out who was winning within the chaos.

Something hit the door with enough force to rock the dresser, dipping the house in a silent nothingness as the fierce combat died into nothing in an instant. Emily and Annabelle sat in silence for a few seconds, awaiting the fate of whoever would come to the door, when the doorknob began to wiggle.

"Butch?" Annabelle cooed, motioning to stand when Emily stopped her. She wordlessly shook her head, wide eyes conveying all they needed to as Annabelle coddled back into their corner, wrapping her body around Emily's.

"Guys? Guys, I'm scared," Gal's voice creaked under the door, entirely void of any emotion like a simulation or an echo.

13

— · —

HANGOVER

"WELL, THEY'RE BACK AT least," Atari murmured, pulling into the driveway.

"They still aren't answering their phones, though."

"Yeah..." Atari's head slowly shook, his tongue grazing his teeth thoughtfully. "You're not feeling good about this either, are you?"

"Oh, we're dead, most certainly," Cass spoke in a halfhearted jest.

Cass went to step out of the car when Atari reached around her, pulling her door shut. "Stay here, just for a few. Just while I go check the place out." He tried to sound confident, to cull that voice in his head that almost begged her to come along.

"But—"

"Just...trust me, okay?"

Atari shifted, stepping out of the car and walking a few paces towards the house before stopping, his fingers running anxiously through his hair. He shuffled in place, pulled by both his will to go for-

ward and his want to go back. He sighed, "Fuck it."
He backtracked, returning to the car and cutting
off Cass's questioning eyes before her voice could
follow. "The glove box," he gestured, "Just reach
into the glove box for me, okay?"

Cass reached in, withdrawing a slick, metallic pistol and Atari tried not to flinch at the disappointed
look that fluttered through her eyes. "You have a
fucking gun?"

"Just...hand it over, please."

Cass weighed their options, passing off the gun
as reluctantly as Prometheus gifting fire, sealing her
fate with a single phrase. "We're talking about this
later. And I'm coming with you."

Atari opened his mouth to argue, the weight of
the gun rooting him to his spot, but Cass was already
passing him and making her way towards the house.
He followed. Cass rammed her shoulder into the
door, pushing as hard as she could, "There's something propped against the door—"

Atari shoved his shoulder into the frame, pushing
on the bending wood as something blocked the
innards of the house. He braced himself for what
they'd find, giving a final bash as the door creaked
open and forced entry as something fell into their
line of sight. Butch's body fell to the ground with
no attempt to stop the fall, splashing into a pool of
crimson that leaked from a multitude of slashes that
carved the body.

His skull was splintered and chunks of viscera still
clung in stringy sinews on the door, almost as if it

had been bashed repeatedly against it. Somehow, Atari didn't scream. Nor did he seem to have the capability of doing so as he eyed the disfigured corpse, almost as if his lungs had been stolen from him.

He fought the urge to run, to jump away, to hide. That desperate, greedy urge that would leave the others to suffer the same grim fate if it meant preserving what little sanity he had left. Still, his mind focused solely on protecting Emily and Annabelle. Atari and Cass clung to the wall. The instinct to keep away from the body so strong that his knees wobbled in defiance as they passed it and entered the house, a new alien sense overtaking the formerly comforting abode. He rimmed the room, making it to the end where it met the hall where he finally peeled his eyes off the body, vomiting into a corner while Cass still clung tight to him.

Atari's shaking hand slid into his pocket, withdrawing his phone and passing it off to Cass. "Try calling them again," he said, wiping chunks of vomit off his lips with his sleeve. Cass took the phone, dialed, and waited. A phone buzzed in response, somewhere in another room, and just as the phone sprang to life, so did the banging. Hit after hit ricocheting throughout the house in a dizzying off-kilter beat that made Atari's entire body tense.

His fear finally pushed to such a feral edge that the mere existence of his body seemed to cut off any other response than to push forward. He crept deeper into the bowels of the enigmatic beast and felt that same tugging in his gut that he'd experience whenever his body got the urge to jump in front of a car. That same ringing in his ear, urging him to catapult himself into the street. To end it all in a final blaze. He knew this, knew how much he feared this version of himself that was drawn to the call of the void as he continued further still, guided by the smooth feel of steel in his grip.

He spun a corner, eyes catching the light, and saw his friend Gal, hanging upside down from the door, making like a rock climber on its sheer face as his limbs seemed to cling to nothing. His head hit the door, over and over, a geyser of crystalline blood flowing from his skull at an increasingly rapid rate as it slammed into a section of the door, splintering both as monotonous as a metronome. The pit of Atari's stomach matched each stroke of the pendulum swing. Cass gasped.

Gal's head swiveled on an impossible axis, ignoring anatomy as the bones ground and ligaments snapped, spiraling his head one hundred eighty degrees and his entire face was crushed, nose entirely flattened, and cheekbones jutting out of bloody clumps of what used to be a functional face. Blood oozed from every orifice, crying just as much of it as he spat.

Gal screamed, though his mouth had been ripped off, the exposed muscles pulsating. A replica of Butch's voice chortled from the being, a leading track accompanied by the screams of Cass and

Emily, all coming from the same gaping, vacuous hole.

"Gal..." was all Atari could muster as he eyed down his friend, feeling the tears permeate down his cheeks. What was he even looking at?

The phantom Gal dropped from the wall, flopping into his own puddle of crimson mush which splashed up around him, before raising on all fours like some demented hound. His destroyed frame hissed, a steamy layer of ichor drowning the gurgling of what could almost be perceived as pleas for help before the beast charged them, skittering down the hall on sloppy limbs.

Atari pulled the trigger, before his mind made the decision, before it could even comprehend what was happening. He fired. The bullet splintered Gal's shoulder, throwing his body backwards but not stopping his rampage as he galloped across the room. Atari found himself screaming, bellowing down the sight as he fired off another round which further cratered his friend's skull. The body skid across the ground another yard, limbs flailing against each other, before coming to a stop just at Atari's feet. He squeezed his eyes shut, awaiting a death that never came. Instead, the clump stayed in its heap, motionless.

Atari's heart fluttered. That same disappointment as whenever a car would pass without his mangled corpse on its grille. That strange, otherworldly sense that he had to abandon his skin if he was going to breathe. He knew these suicidal ideations were merely intrusive thoughts, but that didn't stop the image of his own corpse from flashing before his eyes. A visual impression of Gal pouncing on him and ripping out his innards burned into his eyelids. He stood there, just stood there. Unbreathing. Unblinking.

Unable to process anything at all until Cass's hand took his, a comforting grasp that urged him forward into the abyss of a blood splattered hallway. They crept over the body, Atari's eyes hovering for as long as his mind could handle before shifting his focus back on the busted in door.

He continued, led by a body that acted of its own volition, waves of nausea pounding throughout his being. His hand pushed on the door, which didn't budge, so he pried the hole open the rest of the way. He peeked through and was filled with immediate relief when he saw Emily and Annabelle huddled in the corner, Em rocking in Anna's arms, both wearing petrified eyes but alive.

His eyes took them in. Em wrapping her pinky finger so tightly around Annabelle's that both of theirs were turning purple.

14

Emily's Lament

Past

"THOUGHT I'D FIND YOU out here," Annabelle slung herself over the guiding grip of a wooden railing as rain dripped from the outskirts of the porch light. She wore a crop top and baggy, expansive jeans that swept the floor in dramatic swishes. "You know we have a pool out back if you were planning on getting your legs all soaked, anyway." She sipped from her cider, sloshing it a bit on her drunken lips.

"I just wanted a minute alone," Emily sulked. She poked her feet out into the muddy grass, allowing her thick combat boots to sink a little from their own weight. Her dress sponged up the water that kicked off her knees.

"Is that all you wanted?"

"Are you here to harass me?"

Silence for a moment. Annabelle inspected the moon, almost like she was trying to count the pin-pricks that peppered its surface. "Why would I?"

"You're his friend, right? I'm sure he's told all of you by now. Thomas already hates me." she stifled a sob. "I heard him talking to Cass. He- he called me a bitch. That's why you're here, right?"

"I'm here because I saw a drunk girl leave a party at four in the morning in Pennsylvania," Annabelle spoke slowly, an almost relaxing breeze flowing throughout her cadence. "I'm here because I don't trust frat boys. I'm here because I flunked one too many tests to be indoctrinated into any of the good colleges."

Emily felt a hand graze her shoulder, then felt Annabelle's body plop down beside her, the puddle underneath them shifting to the newcomer. Emily felt the tears she had been choking down explode with the drop of Annabelle's next line. "I'm here because you looked like you needed a friend."

Emily found herself folding, her neck craning so that it rested on Annabelle's shoulder as tears speckled her shirt with the same ferocity as the ensuing raindrops. "You know, I used to wish I was dying, just so the attention was on me. I remember this one friend growing up. We were real close. She had a sister that died while we were in second grade. Drowned, I think. Some kind of accident at a beach where she went into a seizure in the water. I don't remember if I ever knew the details. That Christmas we were really poor, and I remem-ber all I wanted was the new gaming system be-cause mine was so old, and when the holiday rolled around my friend, she got so many toys. She got that gaming system, plus so much more. I remember thinking, why couldn't I have had a sister, just so she could die, and I could finally have the newest stuff?" She poked at the mud some more, making a small, frowning face with her shoe before kicking the access off.

Another pause while she caught her breath. "I'm a horrible person, aren't I?"

Annabelle was silent, and Emily took that as all the response she needed. "It's okay to say it. Trust me, I've said it enough to myself. I broke him. Adam he- he's hurting, isn't he?"

"He is," Annabelle stated. Just that. Stated. There was no anger in her voice, nor resentment. It was almost as if she had no emotions at all, just a void Emily could bounce herself off of.

"This isn't something he'll bounce back from, not anytime soon. I knew that, but I had to, Anna, I just had to—"

"You did."

"I did! And I- and I- I did?"

"I didn't come out here to harass you, and I didn't come out here to say you made the wrong choice either." Annabelle jammed her elbow slightly into Emily's ribs. "I did come out here to offer you a drink to make washing down your decision a bit easier."

Emily's stunned eyes bounced from Annabelle to the drink, testing if it was a secret plot to poison her. "You really don't think I made the wrong choice?"

"I don't think there are any wrong choices in life. We get choices, then we deal with what follows, then we get choices again. It's that simple. I believe you made a choice that's going to hurt my friend. But no, I don't believe you made the wrong choice. Adam, he's a lot stronger than he seems. I know he can come across as brittle. The BPD causes such drastic shifts that it's hard to tell what he is and isn't capable of some days, but I've seen him recover from much worse. It makes him strong too. He's bounced back from things that'd cripple me."

"I broke his heart—"

"He's in his twenties. You're not the first and you're certainly not going to be the last to do that. Besides, no offense, I never saw you two being 'the one' and all that jazz. Whatever cosmically aligns people, you two just didn't have it, no matter how many times he tried to convince himself you did."

"We were on entirely different planes of existence..." Emily caught herself explaining, her voice trailing off.

"You were. I saw what he wanted. I sensed what you didn't."

There was another bloated pause. Emily sobbed.

"You don't do well with goodbyes, do you?" Annabelle snickered.

"I don't do well with hellos. They need to be coaxed out of me like parasites," Emily moaned from the crook of Annabelle's neck. "Goodbyes are infinitely more painful."

Another bout of nothing.

"You really don't think I made the wrong decision?" Emily asked, pleading to be reassured.

"I really don't," Annabelle responded genuinely.

Emily held a shaking hand to where she thought Annabelle's face might be. "Pinky promise?"

A chuckle before a finger closed around hers. "Pinky promise."

"So, what do I do?" Emily pleaded.

"What have you always done?"

"I don't know."

Annabelle raised her cup. "More of that."

15

— · —

SPLITTING

PRESENT

"ATARI, ARE YOU GONNA tell us where the fuck we're going at any point?" Annabelle moaned from the back seat of the van; her body squashed against boxes in a mangled sort of disposition.

"Away." Atari blinked, the vision of his friend's torn skull exploding over and over in his mind, playing at such a deliberate crawl that he could see the eyes rocket out of their sockets, chunks of bone perforating and enveloping the air like bloody snowflakes. Every time he closed his eyes, he was back there, a length of cold steel extending his body outward. His finger itched the leather wheel incessantly, the same motion as pulling the trigger.

Trigger.

His friend was dead while his other friend lay in the hospital dying. At the moment, he was unsure which fate was worse.

He blinked again, squeezing his eyes for a second too long, and had to slam the brakes to avoid hitting another car. "Atari, we can't just fucking leave!"

"Why not? Why not try to leave while we can?"

"Because we have lives—"

"This thing isn't going to stop until we're all dead, Anna. All of us. The same as Trigger. The same as-as- the same..."

"And go where?"

"As far as we can. Wherever we can." Atari's eyes welled up with tears, blinding him as he swerved around a slower pa-diddle, some ancient sort of car that careened around the double lines.

"The Atari I know doesn't just run," Annabelle pleaded.

Atari swung the wheel, breaking as soon as he hit the shoulder. The van lurched to a stop, almost sending Cass and Emily sprawling as they clung to their spots. "All I fucking do is run!" Atari spat, slamming both fists into the wheel. "All I've ever known how to do is run. From relationships, from friends, from myself. It's my programming."

"Atari—"

"I'm not fucking losing anyone else, Anna. I can't keep doing this. I can't. I- I killed Gal, not you, not anyone else. I did. Me."

"He was dead before you—"

"Before I what? Before I shot him in the fucking skull. We don't know that he was dead. We don't know anything. All we know is there's blood on my hands, under my fingernails, and I can't just scrape that shit off." Atari slammed his shoulder into the driver's side door, not bothering to check for other cars as he stepped outside, stumbling through a haze down a roadside hill until his legs collapsed, knees pushing into the grass like the ground was attempting to devour him, to seal him within a coffin of needles.

He screamed incoherent curses into the sky. The dam that usually held his tears at bay broke completely. He vaguely heard the other doors opening, then slamming shut. The twenty feet between them seemed to spread across miles as his ears refused to take in any sound other than his own inhuman wails.

After a while, a hand brushed his shoulder, lightly gripping the back of his neck the way Em always used to. "Adam—"

"Atari," he stifled his sobs just long enough to sigh. 'Please, I'm begging you. Atari." A moment's silence, then he continued. "You wanna know the truth about me? When I was born, I was born with this-this big red button in my brain. One that I always knew I was going to press. This big red self-destruct button that would just...poof...end it all. When we separated, I tried and failed to push that button."

His eyes flickered to Cass, stating, "You wanna know why I had that gun? I bought it after the breakup. Had it stored under my bed this entire time trying to build up the courage to use it. To finally push that fucking button. About a month ago, I drove up to this- this overlook. The one we used to go to, Em. And I sat on the edge of the cliff, eyeing down the sunset and I finally told myself it would be my last one. That I could let go. Finally, be...wherever else, as long as it wasn't here. I sat there for hours with a fucking pistol pressed against my head, just waiting for my hand to finally pull the trigger. And I got fucking close. For the first time in my pitiful life, I got fucking close...then a family pulled up to the parking lot. Some...kids hopped out of the car, and I knew I couldn't in front of them. I snuck the gun back into my glove box and it's been there ever since, waiting for me.

"You wanna know the type of man I am? When we split and I failed to push that button, I realized that maybe I could not push it by killing myself first before it could. That maybe if I ran far enough, fast enough, I could get away from myself. I killed the version of me that truly felt anything so I could hide from it. So yeah, it's just a name to you, but it's more than that to me. It's more than an identity, even. It's about being more than just a countdown until I finally press that button."

He waited for someone, anyone, to speak, and when nobody did, he continued. "I even OD'd once. I never told anyone. I was young, stupid...unmedicated. Hell, at the time, even undiagnosed. Sometimes I think, if the pills had taken me that night, I never would've known what it was like to have been loved. And sometimes that seems like a better option than being, whatever the hell this is, because it isn't living. Now my friend is gone, and my other is going soon, and I'm losing everything I have left."

Emily bent down beside him, staring into his eyes, and he craved nothing more than to wipe the tears from her face. "You know," she croaked, "When we broke up, I never told you why. I had this day; it was a stupid day. Some boomer harassed me at my work, making these advances on me and then screaming when I didn't reciprocate. Then some jerk cut me off in traffic on the drive home. A bunch of small things, y'know. The kinda day where everything just builds off the last. And when I got home, I went to tell you about it and then I just...didn't. I knew you'd want to solve things, that you'd want to be my savior. Always that, always the hero. And I didn't need that. So, when I got home, I let you start talking, and you brought up another idea for some big, flashy wedding. The kind I never wanted. And as you were talking about all these minute details, the color of the cake, the songs to play, who you'd invite. I realized at that moment that you had our entire future planned out and when I looked into it, I'm sorry Ada- Atari, but I saw nothing. Blank, just-blank."

She continued, "You know, in grade school, I grew boobs before anyone else in my class. I was stuffed in a bra before most girls had their first zit. And all these women around me. My mom. My grandma. Teachers. They'd all say, 'That one right there, she's gonna be a heartbreaker. Always that. Never just pretty, they'd always follow it up with 'You were born to break hearts.' Never 'You were born to get a happy ending.' Because they couldn't even fathom love as a fairy tale. I was born to be a bitch, as foretold by my own mother. Breaking people was always my legacy. When I ended things with you, it was never that I didn't love you or I didn't love being with you. It's that whatever it was just wasn't right."

"Why the fuck would you tell me that now?"

"Don't you get it, Atari? I was never going to be the one for you. This...person you have built up in your head, these memories, they're not me. And Atari, you're a good man, you came to save me. You always wanted to save me. To be the hero. But now I'm not the one that needs saving, you have to save yourself first. Look at me," she grabbed both his shoulders, turning him to face her, so they were eye to eye and for the first time Atari's gut fought off her embrace. "You need to stop running from yourself. We need to figure this thing out and you need to stop counting Thomas out of this fight. He's in the hospital right now, fighting for us. How dare we not fight for him?"

"I just...I just don't know what to do, Em, I don't—"

"I might." All heads turned towards Annabelle.

16

THE DEALER

PRESENT

"WHAT DO YOU MEAN?"

"You said it yourself. You guys got a name, right? Hamilton Hanson?" Annabelle chirped, her mind veering in a thousand different directions as her eyes lit up.

"We got an alias. It was a dead end. I don't think Ethel's ever even met the guy. They seem to communicate solely through the phone and delivery points—" Cass began.

"Exactly. So, we trail Ethel to the next point, then camp there long enough that he drops something else off, then we follow him home and bam, we've got our mark."

"That'll take too long," Atari croaked, "We don't have that kinda time if this- this thing following us catches up. We don't know what it'll do next."

"But!" Cass cooed excitedly, "But wait! It's a two-way stream, right? He delivers the product, Ethel sells it, then Ethel must transfer a cut of the money back to him at some point, right? What if we convince Ethel to give us her phone somehow? Then all we need to do is contact him faking a drop-off and case the joint afterwards when we know he'll be showing up?"

"And how are we gonna convince Ethel to give us her phone and let us do that? She was barely willing to give up her client's alias before."

"We could blackmail her," Annabelle shrugged, an almost laughable air of nonchalance in her voice.

"We don't have any dirt on her—"

"We don't," Annabelle stressed, "but Trigger does."

"What do you mean?" Atari asked, trying to rack his brain of any dirt his friend might have on the strange girl from earlier. What did Trigger know that they didn't? Anything would help at this point, and he was desperate for answers.

"Trigger was drunk a while ago and he told me about this party he went to with Ethel and a few others," she proclaimed confidently.

"So?"

"So, he showed me videos he took, and they were all snorting coke. At the time I reprimanded him, of course, but he should still have the videos on his phone. You know how he never deletes anything off that monster. All we have to do is get into his phone and show Ethel the videos, and she'll be eating out of our hands."

"You're evil," Cass laughed in a way that almost mocked genuine emotion.

"You like it," Annabelle smirked.

THE FOUR REMAINING PARTY members crashed their way into the hospital, through the endless labyrinth of monotonous off-white walls spackled with avant-garde abstract art, and past a collection of stuck statuesque people, various patients awaiting anything of value they could use to assess their current situations. They practically ran towards the ICU unit and into Trigger's room, where he laid, just as motionless as before. The tubes and belts and pylons keeping his body together looking like some sort of twisted science experiment.

Atari walked through the wires that snaked across the floor, then rummaged through Trigger's bag of belongings until he fished out his phone. He clicked it open and was surprised to see his own face reflecting back in the light. Trigger's lock screen was a portrait of all of them, laughing and smiling together on some day Atari didn't remember. His eyes bounced between whimsical, happy faces, finally landing on Gal.

Gal. His heart somersaulted seeing his friend once more. His mind flickering between the image and Gal's exploded head like a projector stuck between two frames overlapping the carnage with the familiar.

"What's wrong?" Cass hissed, causing his entire body to jump.

"N-nothing." He reached down, grappling for Trigger's arm, careful to maneuver around the string of bandages that cloaked his body, and pressed his fingertip into the sensor. Relief hit as the phone unlocked, presenting another image of Trigger and his sister at a young age. He quickly shuffled through, rotating to the images and entering the first folder. He hovered for a second, feelings of breaking his friends' privacy bouncing throughout him, but decided it was best to continue.

Atari knew what he'd see; a cobbled together concoction of memes, dick pictures, memories of all sorts, and an incredibly large amount of Em photos. He eventually found what he was looking for, showing the group and they took off with the phone, preparing for the next step as Atari lingered behind, telling them he'd catch up in a minute.

He stood beside Trigger's bed for a while, just looking at his friend as spiderwebs of tubing penetrated his body, keeping him from seeming human and instead presenting itself as something uncanny. Just something taking up residence in the atoms that had once been his friend's body. He pulled up a chair, sitting with a slow creak in his knees, and rested his head on Trigger's chest, feeling his chest rise and fall.

How many more days could he keep up the act that he was okay? Keep acting as though his friend wasn't nearly dead? Keep living with the guilt of all the times he had ignored or hurt his friend in the past? Everything bubbled up now, and before he knew it, a river of tears began running down his face, staining his friend's clothes.

He felt Trigger's chest slowly rise and fall, and within it, his entire being funneled in all his hope, praying to a slew of gods he didn't believe in on the fraction of a chance that any would listen to his pleas. When was the last time he had prayed?

When he could no longer stomach being human, he decided to bottle up his emotions once more, burying them deep within his chest and using any other thought he could muster to drown out their tyranny. He wiped his face and decided to rejoin the others.

"You good?" Cass asked.

"Good."

"ARE YOU SURE HE'S going to be here?" Atari wiggled in a crouching position.

"Yeah, he'll be here. Ethel said so herself," Cass croaked.

"Why do we trust her again?"

"Because we blackmailed her?"

"Yeah, but why would she be so adamant not to share any actual info and then suddenly rat him out? I don't know, I'm just not buying it."

"Both of you, shut up. This is a fucking stakeout."

"Don't say stakeout like we're secret agents."

The four bickered back and forth, staring at the innocuous black lockbox that rested with the wavering shadows of some back alley. "Are we sure this is even the right spot?" Atari whispered.

"Wait, is that a flashlight?" Annabelle smacked Atari on the leg.

A single light illuminated the alley, just strong enough for someone to be able to find their footing in the dense expanse of night. Whatever it was bobbed lightly. They snuck up to the box, plucking it off the ground and holding it up to the light, where a hand fumbled for the combination. Atari and Cass snuck out of the car, surrounding him and blocking off either escape route. The man spun, caught by surprise as Atari held out a hand like he was hushing a dog. "We just wanna talk-"

The lockbox was flung at Atari's head, his arms barely deflecting it. The man's head whipped around and, upon realizing he was surrounded, made a mad dash straight towards Atari. Atari readied his stance, but to no avail. His opponent swung their body with such force that it threw him off his feet. He cracked his head on the wall, immediately seeing spots as the other man fumbled from the impact, spiraling into a few trash bags where his legs flailed through garbage. He stood wobbly. One foot caught on the trash, and as he shook it free, he launched some of it into the air.

He was about to get away when Atari screamed, "I took it! The Kronos! I took Kronos!" Unsure what he was expecting, but the man stopped, looking back over his shoulder, and for the first time Atari saw his face, a look of extreme pity etched into it.

TWO SHAKING HANDS CARRIED a tray full of drinks to the table, spilling a bit of their contents as a voice whimpered, "I'm sorry- I know it don't mean much, but I am sorry."

"So, let's just get this straight," Atari said, ignoring the drinks and stabbing into the table with his hands. "These pills, they're—"

"Interdimensional, yes. What are you not getting here?" Annoyance seeped deep into Hamilton's voice.

"Because they're infused with some kinda creature?" Cass continued, just as bewildered.

"It's ichor, holy ichor, now if I could just continue and—"

"And since we took it, time's acting irrationally?" Annabelle questioned.

"No, time isn't altered. Are you people even listening to me?" the man wailed, his voice scratchy and erratic like an old record, skipping around syllables as he croaked. "Listen, what is wrong with you people? You have to understand the immediate threat you're all in! Now listen. It's blood. The pills, they are made of its blood. Like the big 'It', capital 'G' kinda God. You're not seeing the future or the past, you're simply not seeing time. It's beyond such concepts. It's like this." He drew a straight line across a layer of dust coating the table.

"We see time as this- this fucking line, alright? You get stuck in an endless pattern of past, present, future. Everything is either a memory or yet to come, right?"

He blew on the table, spraying the dust particles into the air where a thin beam of light caught them, his eyes bouncing between sections of flaking snowflakes like his brain was trying to peer inside of them. "Now, picture time as more like that! Billions upon billions of instances happening simultaneously, a web of interconnecting segments that could be traveled on a whim. One where you're both seven and twenty, dead and back, so long as you're one consciousness, you're free to visit any point in that existence. That's 'It.'"

"So, what, I take the pills, go back in time and stop myself from ever taking the pills in the first place?" Atari mumbled in disbelief at his own words.

"You're not understanding me," the man sighed. "There is no 'back' with time. There is no 'changing the past' because there is no past to speak of! The only thing for certain is that each of these moments, each and every particle of dust, they're all happening. Right now. And right now. And so on and so forth, forever and eternity." He exhaled for possibly the first time.

"You'll only ever be going forward in time, even when you go back. That just means that what you experienced is now going to be a future, and that's what's so fucked up about it all. About "It" all, man."

"And how the fuck did you acquire the blood of a god, then?" Annabelle mocked.

His face scrunched up as if the question disgusted him. "How does anybody?" He tapped the table vigorously. "I'm a Messiah!" He paused for a second. "Yeah, laugh it up. Assholes. People probably laughed at Jesus' disciples too and look where that got them."

He grabbed his drink, taking a swig. "Listen, you've already seen shit that can't be explained. You came in here talking about seeing the future and being chased by a demon and offing your buddy after a possession. That's some shit. What's one more turd for the pile?"

"The analogy meaning?"

"You're royally fucked. Once you see the thing, there's no going back. I found out through my own eyes that once you take the pills, it sinks its teeth into you, eventually."

"What happened to you?" Annabelle gawked.

"It started with me and my buddies. We got together all the time, under the bridge, ya know, and we were just having fun, shooting shit. My one buddy, Cynthia, reaches into her pocket and pulls out a small baggie. She tosses it to me and asks if I wanna try one. I've never backed down, so I take one and then I'm reeling over in pain. Then," he snapped, "just like that, I'm back to being a child. Only I'm not in control of my body anymore, it's just...moving. I'm running around my childhood house and giggling like crazy and my mom's there. I haven't seen my mom since she passed years ago, but she's right there in front of me and all I wanna do is hold her and tell her I love her but instead I'm whizzing around the house shitting myself."

He paused for a second, face getting closer as he leered over the drinks. "Only then I see something out the corner of my eye and I'm instantly entranced. It's just there. Just staring. And it's beautiful. But this visage of God it followed me when I returned to the bridge. It hasn't left my side since. Cynthia killed herself two days later. Then Jack. Then Marshall. Each one unveiling more clues to what was actually happening and by the time I really figured it out, it was too late. I was the last one from that bridge."

"Then why continue to spread them?"

"Because that's what happens when you do keep it at bay. When you let it feast with little sacrifices. Give it, its- its virgins or what have you. This thing we're dealing with, it's Lovecraftian, it's old- possibly the oldest thing. It could end all of reality if it wanted to, just like-" he snapped his fingers, "-that."

"How do you know all this?"

"Because that's what 'It'- the 'Elder God' showed me when I took the fucking pills! I saw it all, clear as day. Everyone. Everything. All of it, just gone. If the beast is starved, there's nothing but death. That's what I saw, same as you saw your girl over there swinging from the rope. That's what I was chosen to stop! God's blood gave me the gift of sight to save the world and I'm so sorry you had to fall in the line of it, but that's simply how it has to be. You and your friend were chosen, same as me, and it's my cross to bear and—" a fist flung at the man's face, knocking him against the wall and even Atari looked shocked at the might of his swing.

"That's our friend dying! That thing got to him because you let it! You purposefully sold it to him, and for what? You sick fuck!" Atari screamed, lining up another blow and piling it into the man. His knuckles stung with the impact, tremors of hairline fractures forming in them.

Atari reared back, his body ready for another blow, when Emily's hand shot out, the lighter skin on her palm flagging him down. "Wait, wait, wait. Atari, stop."

Atari had to fight back the red in his eyes. His fist almost flinging straight through her, and he had to recoil at the thought of hurting her. He looked at the bloodied man, at what he had caused, but felt no remorse, only a further lust to smash in the man's skull. "Why should I?" he hissed.

"Because he's the only one that could help us," Cass croaked from the side somewhere outside Atari's tunnel vision. "Because he knows more than us, Atari. He's taken the pills, he's seen the creature, and he's still alive. He could be valuable." Cass shot a glance at the pitiful pile of blubbering man. "That's the only reason I'm not killing him myself."

Hamilton rose on his elbows, still clutching his face. "Persecute me all you want. The only crime I've committed is saving the world. If you- children- can't see that, then that's on you."

Atari's fist slammed the table before he was even aware of his actions. "If you so much as speak out of turn again, I'll feed you your own tongue," Atari hissed. His mind flooded with a renewed vigor that overtook his entire body. "What about you? You took the pills. How come Gal is dead and you're still alive?"

"The pills. They're not what you think they are. They're a catalyst, that's all. Ingesting divine blood will show you things you could never imagine, but it comes at a price. You taking the pills simply put you and your loved ones on its radar. It chose to spare me," he licked his lips, regret flooding through his teary eyes, "It didn't offer the same courtesy to my friends. Don't you dare treat me like I don't know what loss is. You haven't seen loss, not yet. Not until you're staring at the corpse of your last remaining lifeline. Not until you're borderline inhuman. Then, and only then, will you be able to judge me. But you won't- if it decides to spare you- you won't be any better than me."

Atari faced the scared looks on his friends' faces, his stance switching from offensive to defensive. Was this really his fault? Could he bear that burden? "I am," he finally said, laying emphasis on every word. "Better than you. I am. And if you're not gonna help us stop this thing, then you can fuck off."

"You still don't understand, do you? There is no 'stop this'. There is only you and your friends dying a gruesome death at the hands of fate. That's how it starts, that's how it spreads and infects. First you see it. Then it works its way into your loved ones' heads. They start to see it too, even without taking the pills. It takes them too. Only it's smart, it knows it needs to keep going, keep eating and all that, so it only takes what it needs and then it lies low. But hear me kids, the only reason there's a human race left is because this God allows there to be. You're already dead. Not just your girl, all of you. The only, and I do mean, only way to be spared, is to surrender yourself as its vessel and put as much distance as you can between you and your friends. To become like me and help it spread and then pray that it spares you. That's the extent of your lives now, death or servitude-"

Atari stood, pushing out on the table so the drinks clattered around him. "We're leaving." The other three stood, glaring at the pathetic man, Annabelle wrapping her arms protectively around Atari's shoulders as they began for the door.

"If you're smart, you'll live," the man called out. "At the very least, as long as it lets you. There's nothing after we die. It showed me that. Its blood showed me that. Nothing but black, nothing but—" They slammed the door behind them.

17

— · —

HAUNTED

PRESENT

HAMILTON HANSEN WATCHED THE kids leave, one after the other, storming out into the intense rays of sun that enveloped them whole. He watched the door slam shut and devour that same sun, drowning his house once again in a darkness as palpable as the quiet that followed their departure. It took him a bit to stand and even longer to figure out what to do with the movement. He grabbed for the tray of drinks, all of which were still full besides his own, and found his legs heading into the kitchen to dump them out.

He found himself peeking out every window, as if daring the kids to return, to allow the hot-headed one to finish what they had started on his face. His face. He figured he should grab an ice pack while he was in there, if not out of necessity, than out of habit of continuing through life like the human he knew he should be. He dropped the cups beside the sink first, its interior so full of other stacks of dirty dishes that there was no room in there for them. The dirty dishes were becoming self-aware: his stale plates slowly farming sentience he wouldn't be around to see.

He reached his hand into the freezer for an ice pack and, of course, found none; they had already been used and never put back where they belonged. He instead chose an old bag of corn, holding its lumpy surface to the grooves of his face, instantly soothing the pounding a bit, lightening up on the burning too. He circled the house a few times, a hobble in his legs as he unmasked, relaxing the tension that had built up in it. He paraded around each room like a ghost, never making so much as an imprint. He checked every window for any signs of movement. Hamilton entered one room and froze for a split second, seeing something out of the corner of his eye.

A body appeared in the corner of the room where it sprawled out in a rag-doll pose, slit wrists profusely bleeding. He saw its face vividly against the floor, rising from the pool of blood in a silent scream. Her eyes gouged out by an infinite number of jagged incisions, as if someone had carved them out in a wild frenzy. The skin around the empty sockets had already begun to bloat, a purplish hue setting in and mixing with the sloshing crimson. Then, just as suddenly, the figure disappeared, an empty space caught in the light as if it had never been there.

His racing heart crescendoed as he passed the spot, turning his back on the emptiness with a jagged sort of fear that made his hair stand on end. He scampered away, squeezing his eyes shut and shaking his head to try to ward off the hallucinatory sleepiness that he blamed the sight on.

When his eyes reopened, he was in hell. The house had decayed, pillars of wall fragments stretching a few feet up into nothingness as if the house had been hit with a bomb. The outside world sat just outside its parameters, acting more as a gate than the house it had been seconds before.

The worst part about being able to see outside was the bodies. Hundreds of them, littering the streets and yards, hanging out of cars, and peppering the remains of neighboring buildings. Clusters of bodies that stretched as far as Hamilton could see. Some had obvious wounds, gored stomachs or slit wrists or bashed in skulls. The rest looked pristine, as if they had just dropped dead out of nowhere. Hamilton struggled to get his shaking legs to walk past the perimeter of the house and out into the streets.

Silence. An absolute, all-consuming silence. Not a thing moved besides him, no animals made a sound, no cars rang out among the corpses. He closed his eyes, counting to ten over and over again in his mind.

One, two, three—

He stepped over a corpse that wore another friend's face; their mouth sewn shut with a silver fishing wire type material, their pale face juxtaposing how blue their lips had become.

Four, five, six—

He ducked under a line of feet, dangling in the air. The black girl, Emily, hung from a rope that strung out towards the sky, her neck crammed in a crooked angle and foam still leaking from her lips.

Seven, Eight, Nine—

He knew he had to wake up. That he had to tear his mind from the place before it stole his sanity in its entirety. He prayed to return to his home. To finally be free of the vision that had haunted him since taking those pills.

Ten.

He was back in his home, his real home, as if nothing had happened. Only when he tried to move did he feel a deep pain sear through him. He looked down at his body, which seemed on forever, as if he had lost all depth perception, and noticed another drop of crimson hit the ground, spraying off his fingertips.

His wrists had been slit. Gashes tugged through the skin with pinpoint precision, a straight line nicking every vein in its path. He felt the nausea hit with the same intensity as the pain, thrumming more vigorously by the second as he flung his body against the wall. He took a step forward and felt another jolt while a series of crunches sprang to life. He lifted his foot, and a collection of jagged ornate glass punctured it. The same that must've slit his wrists.

He used the wall as a crutch, guiding his body absently from room to room, not really sure what he was looking for as a trail of blood oozed out behind him. He stumbled, slipping in his blood, and fell face first into the puddle of coagulated ichor. He attempted to stand, but the pain in his wrists grew too unbearable to put that much pressure on. His head whipped around the room, the shadows twirling in an aggressive wave.

He watched, pain distilled through fear as the shadows began to take form, an oil-like ooze combining into a single amalgamation that crept into the full space of the room. It stood impossibly tall; a humanoid frame stretched over the body of a giant whose monstrous neck craned toward the ceiling. Hamilton was far too familiar with the being, with its desperate majesty. Its sleek, featureless body vibrated, gestating in seconds as a tumorous lump crawled from under its taut skin.

It shivered, scurrying like an insect until it reached the point of the being closest to Hamilton where it burst through, forming the rough shape of a face that continuously folded outward until it twisted into a perfect mock visage of his friend Cynthia. She had been the first of his friends to die, the first step to severing his tether on reality, and as she screamed with that animalistic wail she had carried all those weeks ago, he felt a tugging of bile in his gut.

"Harry?" it hissed, and he flinched at hearing his real name. It hadn't been since her death that anyone had called him that. "Harry? Please! It's so dark, Harry!"

The face fractured open, splitting into multiple others as the rest of his deceased friends joined her, wailing in unison. "Harry? Harry? Harry!"

He went to reach out towards them, splattering blood onto his face as it fell from his corroded veins. "I'm here," he shouted. "Please! I'm here. Please don't leave me." His attention switched to the beast's featureless head. "I'm chosen! You can't kill me. I'm chosen!"

18

BEGINNING OF THE END

PRESENT

"So...I'm open to game plans if anybody wants to throw anything out," Cass murmured to the remainder of the group.

"My uncle has a cabin, a very secluded, woodsy type, somewhere far away from other people. We could hole up there for a while—" Emily began.

"This is an interdimensional...thingy or whatever, not one of your ex-boyfriends. I don't think we can just run away from this one," Annabelle groaned.

"I don't run away! And that's not what I meant, okay? I just meant until we come up with something better, we can at least- I don't know."

"At least find ourselves alone and hunted. You saw what that thing did to Trigger when he was-when he was-" Cass shot a glance at Atari, obviously stammering over the word, 'alone.' "Besides, we still don't even know what rules we're playing with. I mean, we don't even really know what that- that thing is. Or why it's doing what it's doing. Or if we can even trust Hamilton's word."

"Well, do you have a better idea? Cause if you do, I'd love to hear it!"

"Guys," Atari mumbled, his voice drowned out in the back and forth.

"I say we go to the most populated area. What's it gonna do if we're at Times Square? Maybe there's strength in crowds," Cass pondered.

Atari slammed the brakes of the van, sending each of the occupants flying against their seat belts. "There is no more plan. You heard him. I'm a poison to be around. I unleashed this thing, and the only way the three of you live is getting as far away from me as possible. That's it. Period."

Cass, Emily, and Annabelle exchanged glances. "Yeah, that's certainly not a possibility," Cass said.

"And just who do you think we are? Do you really think we'd just abandon someone like that?"

"This isn't up for discussion. This is final," Atari huffed, fighting a losing war against them. "I'm serious. For once in my fucking life, I'm entirely serious."

"So are we. I lost my Butch because of this. We all lost Gal. You're right, this is serious. And we're not gonna stop until Kronos is gone."

"Kronos... that's it! Kronos! That's the new plan!"

"What's the new plan?" Emily asked, clearly confused.

"A bad one," Atari croaked. "The pills- Kronos- he said it himself, right? It's God's blood. That's our way of going toe to toe with this thing. We level the playing field." He ripped the bag of capsules from his pocket, counting them out. "We've got nine, ten, twelve, fifteen... fifteen pills in total. If only one lets us see into the future, imagine what all fifteen could do."

"So, your plan is to OD and leave us with the corpse?"

"Who's to say I will? We don't know anything about these things. Odds are I could OD, but this thing's gonna kill us, regardless. If there's even the slightest odds that I could, I don't know, adopt its powers or something. Even a smidge. Transcend to a level where its presence is more physical." He looked at Emily, the shadows cascading around her neck like the noose was already around it. He looked into those eyes, so full of life, and knew he had to protect them. "Shit's about to get serious. If you're stuck on the concept of staying, then I have an idea of where we can do it."

ATARI EYED DOWN THE collection of pills in his hand, their bulk heavy with the weight of memories. His entire body shook feverishly, quaking with anticipation as his hand hefted the pills robotically to an aching mouth. Atari's tongue lapped up the pills as eagerly and familiar as drinking water. His body felt the effects of the pills the second they hit his tongue, the pain spawning in his throat before he even had the chance to swallow. His throat collapsed in on itself, fifteen pills clanging together, bouncing off the sides of his scorched esophagus. Pain. He felt pain in every bone, every muscle, every atom. His world melting into pain and pain alone. At first, he thought he had died and was burning in hell, tortured outside of corporeal capabilities.

He raised a stinging arm, a mixture of sensations as it felt numb and on fire simultaneously. His vision swung like he was hanging from a wind chime, the outline of Emily's house blurring around him like a Dali painting. He tried to focus his fleeting visuals on that staircase, the same one he saw her hanging from every time he closed his eyes. He held onto that sight, grounding himself in reality as the fractals of dissociated time began to spiral into a moving mesh of universes. Nothing. There was nothing he could do to stop the ceaseless waving assault.

He held up his arm and it no longer transcended time but reality altogether, altering between strands of the universe that he simply picked through like sand on the beach. His atoms visibly clashing and separating and combining once more in an intricate display. Then, as his brain threatened to snap entirely, some semblance reemerged, every possible second snapping in like a rubber band.

He opened his eyes and where the streaks of worlds combined formed the endless fractals of jagged brown irises. Emily stared him down, a younger Emily, the markers of years spent apart not quite gestating on her face yet. His mouth muscles moved involuntarily. "Em?"

Emily went to speak, a gargling escaping her lips as an invisible force launched them backwards, rag dolling her body through the air with an intense force. Her body lurched, the movements uncannily human while maintaining that unnatural disposition, until finally her body came to rest, levitating in the air like a slowly swaying pendulum. It was then that Atari noticed the thick layer of rope wrapped around her throat, the chain that must've drug her to that position. Her neck craned to the side, drooping as an entire body's worth of weight held it in the air, bloating the skin around the rope.

Atari stared into her lifeless eyes. Eyes that were devoid of anything at all. Two porcelain globes that greedily mimicked life from within an empty vessel.

Everything Atari ever feared stared him down.

Emily's body began to expand, bones popping as they curled at impossible angles, stretching indefinitely until the features began to blend into its base, spiraling until they stopped existing altogether. Atari watched, abject fear fluttering through his eyes as his old lover morphed, taking on the outline of the creature that had been haunting him, a gaunt, glowering monolith of off-colored flesh that wrapped a stubbornly starving frame.

It crackled, like crunching into an apple as the contorting bones pushed their way through to the brief lighting. He swore he could smell it, though the smell was indefinable to the nose. He watched her lose her eyes to the stretch, first rolling back into her skull before being covered by an expansive cheek bone.

Nothing. He could do nothing as his body froze, uselessly regaining sensation while his bones filled with lead. Finally, painstakingly, he turned, his vision spiraling into sparse shapes until the world reformed around him, Trigger's bloodied body procuring from nothingness. Trigger's limbs were unnaturally long, as if viewed through a fisheye lens and as Atari watched his friend slit his wrists, over and over again, the lacerations healing and then reforming just to bleed out again, spilling onto the patterned floor.

Atari started towards his friend, taking one step before the void swallowed him entirely, spitting him back out into the hall of Annabelle's house. His foot hit the ground just as the scurrying of pounding feet erupted from the ceiling, followed by the visage of Gal crawling upside down, his jaw slack and eyes as lifeless as Emily's. Atari stumbled backwards, realizing he was once again holding the gun within his quivering palm.

His hand spun, pulling the trigger and firing three shots into the air. One hit, pummeling Gal's shoulder, but the corpse barely so much as shivered, the only movement cascading from the rippling force of bullet through muscle as it clung tight to the ceiling. Atari flung himself backward, stumbling around in the darkness as Gal's mandibles split open like a blooming flower, rows upon rows of teeth forming a jagged mountain range on its stem, disappearing into a damp abyss.

Atari watched helplessly as it dropped to the ground in a heap, its body rising on awkwardly bent limbs as it clambered on all fours toward him. He fired again, jumping out of the way just as the beast smashed through the door behind him, disappearing into the room. He ran just as its hands reached through the doorway, clinging hold and pulling itself back into the hall. It chased him, racing him down the hall until he came to a single room that housed Emily and Cass's pleading voices. His voice joined the chorus, reaching a crescendo when the beast reared up before him, easily fending off his desperate assault to escape and grabbing him by the upper and lower jaw.

He felt the beast's fingers curl around his teeth, hitting his gums where they dug in as it began to pull. Atari sobbed as he felt the sinews of muscle holding his jaws together begin to snap, the corners of his mouth splitting open as the Gal replica pulled its hands apart. The bones popped, then ground together for a second before separating as it hoisted Atari in the air, his dangling feet fighting for a ground which never came.

He knew he had to force his way into a different memory before his jaw snapped entirely, but the pain was making it too hard to focus, the dancing lights that flooded his vision sending all other sight spiraling. He spat through pain, his tongue desperately trying to reclaim the roof of his mouth. Just as the pain threatened an episode of all-consuming agony, he found within his vision those dancing fragments of a universe beyond his, sliding between the fabric, and found himself staring at Emily and Cass as they shimmied around a body. His body.

He watched as he laid motionless on the floor, body slumped so weightily that it might as well be sinking into the floorboards. Emily and Cass both panicked, jumping around to different spots in the room when a knock at the door drew the eyes of all three of them, only Atari's doppelgänger body not falling victim to its siren call.

"Who- who is it?" Cass called out, confused.

"This is Officer Mallory with the Pleasant Hills police department. Open the door..."

19

— • —

DEATH OF A FRIEND

PRESENT

EMILY FROZE, HER EYES locking with Cass and Annabelle, all three waiting for something unknown with bated breath. Then the knocking began again, followed by a curt voice at the door. "Police! Open up!"

Annabelle paled as all three shared a glance that immediately displayed their fears. The officers were obviously drawn to the area after discovering the bodies of Butch and Gal in Annabelle's house. Cass was the first to react, bold enough to take a few shuffling steps towards the door before turning back to the others. "What do I say to them?"

"Anything that gets them out of here!" Annabelle moaned.

"How do I do that?"

"Improv? How should we know?" Emily's eyes flickered to Atari's catatonic body lying in the center of the room, then pointed back towards the spiral staircase that split her house, her throat tightening as if she could already feel the coils of rope pressing into her neck.

"I'm sorry I didn't sign up for this demon shit," Cass howled as the banging grew louder. She crawled towards the door, forcing a shaking hand to try the handle, knowing full well what was coming when she opened it. The door creaked open an inch, pried the rest of the way, and two officers stood before her, backlit by a slew of revolving red and blue lights. The first, the taller of the two, was a stout man with a balding patch sprouting from his oversized head, which was probably eight inches higher than his partners, despite the man's obvious hunch. The man shoved his foot in the door, assuring Cass couldn't slam it shut, and began to speak once again, his voice gruff and striking.

"Miss Annabelle Amel, I presume?" Cass's face must've reflected her confusion because he continued, "This is the home of Miss Annabelle Amel, correct?" His voice was calm, stoic, but his finger itched for the release of his pistol. They knew.

"Who's asking?"

"Someone with questions on account of the deaths of Butch Barley and Gale Downey. We caught word from neighborhood sightings that she was in the area and were looking to bring her and her friends in for questioning. Now I'll ask one more time, are you Annabelle Amel?"

"Cassandra Sykes."

"Alright, Miss Cassandra, I'm afraid we're going to have to ask you to come with us and complete a round of questioning."

Cass went to speak when the officer began his advance on the house. "We're coming in—"

"No, thank you." Cass went to slam the door, but the man blocked it with his body.

"I wasn't asking," he commanded as he motioned for the portly man to follow close behind, upholstering his firearm.

Defeated, Cass trailed off a bit, granting them access to the house where they immediately plagued it with an air of investigation, leaning into their guns as they searched each room. Cass knew it would be mere seconds before they found Atari, comatose on the floor, with no explanation as to how he got in such a vegetative state. Cass clawed at the skin on her arms nervously, desperate to call out and warn the others, to somehow telepathically let them know to hide the body.

The jumpy officers paraded through the space between rooms and Cass knew any sudden frenzy would send their reactive bodies into action. The taller one, the leader of the two, approached the door to the living room cautiously, dropping his gun just long enough to pivot inside the space and Cass's stomach sank as they shouted, "Get down with your hands up," into the space.

She hovered behind him, gazing upon the crime scene. Annabelle and Emily both had the sense to duck, raising their arms in a slow and submissive stance. Atari's body laid face up, trapped in an expression of nothingness like Sleeping Beauty. His mouth foamed slightly, if from the pills or drool she couldn't tell. The taller officer snuck up behind Annabelle, patting her down while the other went to check on Atari's body, feeling around for a pulse and nodding to his partner when he found it. He motioned for the radio on his chest, clicking it, and cleared his throat to speak into the static.

Cass, in a moment of blind intuition, flung herself across the room, successfully dive bombing the man who let out a shriek, clawing for his back as Cass swung like an ape, trapping him in a headlock. The two wrangled each other, Cass maneuvering her body around the man's muscular arms, only evening the playing field through the man's blind panic. He caught her leg, swinging into a death roll, and catapulting her body to the rough wood floor where she hit the ground with a meaty thud.

The officer pivoted, pointing his pistol directly at Cass and shouting, "You bitch! Ronny?" He looked towards his partner and Cass took the opportunity to slither to her stomach, attempting to raise when the officer's eyes flashed back at her. "Stay the fuck where you are!"

He took a step forward, immediately tripping over himself as Annabelle shot out an arm, blocking his leg in the darkness. He fumbled forward; the gun sliding across the floor, where it came to a halt a few feet away. The other officer, Ronny, a stout man with wavy hair that faded into rough sideburns, plowed through the center of the room, attempting to regain control of the room by wildly swinging his pistol at anything that moved.

"Quint," he mumbled, reaching out a hand to help his partner up. He took his eyes off the girls for a second, gaining cognizance of where his fumbling hand was in relation to the other officers when Cass and Emily took their chance, Cass diving for the gun on the ground while Emily charged Ronny, using her entire body to pressure his arm to the ground. Ronny's finger tightened, firing shots into the floorboards with such force that they sent a shower of splinters, rocking the entire flooring as each shot perforated through it. Ronny spastically shoved his elbow around a cramped bend in the small space between them as he struggled to raise the weapon above his hip.

He managed to shake off Emily just as Cass tackled the pistol on the floor, rotating it in her hand and pointing it at the officers. She closed her eyes, mentally preparing herself for the damage she was about to do, but the adrenaline had pushed her body so far, it was too late to turn back now. Rimming the trigger with her finger, she twitched, sending fireworks from her wrist as the kickback shot through her bones.

Ronny flung himself to the ground, letting his partner's writhing mass drop once more as Annabelle jumped in to cover Emily's unmoving body. The scene erupted into a shootout, bullet casings dropping to the ground before Cass was even aware she had squeezed off the first shot, carried by survival instinct alone.

Cass knew she wasn't aiming, that she wasn't actually trying to hit the officers, just trying to buy them enough time to figure out another plan. Still, she wasn't not aiming for them either, firing random potshots with the hope that none would cause unnecessary casualties. Her eyes flickered to Annabelle, who was dragging Emily from the room. She turned back, her eyes swinging a bit faster than her head, and never even saw the bullet as it shredded her body, tearing through musculature and shattering bone as it ate away at her very being.

She could feel her organs rearrange, splattering a brownish blood onto the floor in great gouts as her body shambled backwards, surrendering itself to the susurrus of the floor. The floorboards immediately began greedily lapping up her blood, that geysered from her petite frame.

She watched, barely aware, as Annabelle's body flung on top of her, arms sloshing around through the layer of blood-soaked cloth in a clawing attempt to coat the wound in pressure. She watched, barely feeling as her heaving chest showcased her fear, her stomach muscles twisting and contorting like a zombie infected person in a film. She listened, barely able to make out the words that funneled from Annabelle's mouth, as if they came from a million miles away. "Cass? Cass, stay with me!"

Cass could feel every moment, every second, creeping around her like time itself had been enveloped in syrup. She helplessly observed, too buried in her own agony to do more than flail as the officer pinned Annabelle to the ground, pushing the tongue of that life- ending beast in her face as his partner cried something into his chest radio.

Cass knew she was dying, somehow, impossibly, she knew. It came in every breath she took, how they shallowed like waves being drawn back to the sea during low tide. It came in the beat of her racing heart rising in her ear, perforating through the layers of chaos until only it remained. And it came in the thoughts that reflected at her, memories shuffling through her visuals, truly dancing semi-translucent, as if etched on top of reality.

She looked towards Emily's body, and regret poured into her. What would Atari do if he ever found out what they had done? How would he view her? She cursed herself for never telling him herself. She thought about all the ways he'd find out. Everything from the absurdity of him smelling her lingering presence pushed deep within Emily's pores to the more logical answers, like Emily telling him herself. She knew she couldn't stomach the look of betrayal he'd likely give her. She rolled over on her side, back arched, her hands wrenching for her stomach. She could almost feel him wrapped around her. His arms comfortingly warm, the skin on his chest heating up the small of her back.

She listened, past the beating of her heart, and found his voice soothing and calm. "Remember our art project, in Miss. Keilings class? We had to paint the Mona Lisa...remember?" The question. It lingered in her mind, anchoring her to a certain vision of her painting hanging directly beside his. Twin mistakes on the canvas of exploring immortality, a disgusting simulacrum of such intricate design. "But I'll always have you, and that makes me special," Atari's disembodied voice reassured her.

20

THE SACRIFICE

ATARI DROPPED TO HIS knees, watching Cass die as a seizure consumed her, her spastic body throwing off blood onto his unconscious one. Fireworks exploded behind her eyes, a brief explosion of consciousness that gave way to a haze of nothingness. He knew she could neither see nor feel him. Still, he laid behind her, wrapping her in a loving embrace as he felt her body slowly stop functioning, holding on even as his wispy hands caught nothing. Trapped. His body was trapped on the ground.

He waited for her to be gone, completely gone, not even attempting to move as Annabelle was ripped off of her, kicking and screaming, her arms forced behind her back as the one officer reached for his handcuffs. He watched her and Emily get locked into position and painstakingly stood to his feet, ready to continue his mission. He pushed through the waves of time that enveloped the space surrounding him, transferring him to the outskirts of consciousness where he clung to the edge of a ceaseless void. A void he simply registered as 'The End.', His end. Every moment past existing in a space without his presence.

He pushed against the boundary, finding refuge in the last few moments leading up to the vast unknown, readying his mind to interpret what he knew would be the end of his life. When tangibility returned, he found himself within an alien home. He saw a single figure sat in a wheelchair, the man's back towards him as they stared out a window which breached the room in majestic overflowing beams. He crept up on them, each step seeming to take all his effort as he forced his body to continue the motions, his entire being screaming in agonizing fear. The body jerked, and he flinched, then it went calm once more, head lulling to the side.

Atari rounded the figure and saw a twisted version of himself, riddled with age. The weight of all those years bore into his face like a topological map, their power ensnared caustic shadows. Atari, the other Atari, had their eyes wide. Wide and vacant, almost like there was nothing to be had within his reflection. His fingers drew claw marks on the wheelchair's arms, constricting in jerking movements with no discernable pattern. His mouth choked on a thick, bubbling foam that oozed from the side of his lips. Atari called for help, screamed for anyone that would listen before realizing that he wasn't able to make use of his lungs. He waited. Nobody came. Nobody ever would.

He reached out a quivering hand, one that jerked nearly as much as his older self and clawed just as desperately at their fearful hands. Everything. Everything about him was in those hands. Fear in the way they curled. Loneliness in the way they grappled for anything worthy of his holding. His hand went straight through his reflected self, and he remembered that he wasn't on the same plane of existence anymore. Instead, he hovered his hand on top of the dying man's, questioning what he was wasting by doing so. Not his time, not anymore, but his sanity. Still, he refused to leave the man to die alone, even if he technically still was.

Atari stared into his own vacant eyes as they wept silently, still reflecting the sunset in his golden orbs. He held onto those old, scratching hands. "You're not alone," he told himself. "You were never alone." He stayed with himself as he died, both sets of eyes watching the sunset. He knew now what he had to do. He pushed his way through his existence, now traveling with precision as he entered himself, pulling into the moment right before the gun went off, trumpeting Gal out of existence. He eyed his friend as Gal barreled towards him, making great strides across the ceiling in a gallop.

The phantom Gal reached the spot where his gun should've gone off but instead Atari turned around, fluttering his limbs like a matador, just barely side-stepping Gal's pounce. He spun, racing down the hall and out of the house as Gal's footsteps followed, making way for the house he had left with the blonde lady still lying nude inside. The same one he had stored his lighter the first time he had tripped on Kronos. He ran his fingers along the ramshackle wall, waltzing around it until he made it to that brick that was loose, prying it out and revealing a little cubby behind it.

He reached a hand in, delicately pushing the lighter to the back and shoving the pistol inside before spinning around, the scene transitioning with the motion of his spin until he was back inside the decrepit, lonely house where Emily's body swayed.

Her fate, he knew, was to be here. Alone. Swaying like a pendulum in the slight breeze of a mostly stale apartment, rotting until the smell was enough to alert the neighbors. His eyes found the body, for the first time really taking it in. Truly comprehending that this thing was Emily. His body moved. Not on its own will, but not being piloted either. Some third state took over where his consciousness found a new motivation in the tasks.

He walked up to her, swinging above the knocked over stool, and allowed himself sight. Her snapped neck had a bone jutting out, nearly tearing through the skin which swelled around it. Her lips were an icy color, dried out and flaking. Her eyes were wide and lifeless. She somehow both was and wasn't Emily. His body continued forward, taking her body and lifting upward so the noose slackened, then he lowered her to the ground, as gently as possible, given her dead weight.

How many times had he gotten lost in those eyes?

He went back, retrieving the noose and slowly coiling it in his arms, a new weight added to it, heavier than anything it had experienced thus far, almost as if the noose itself knew the task at hand. He went outside, nearly vomiting from the intensity of his beating heart, as he added the noose to the stockpile in the wall, waiting for that red car to show up again.

He reached in, withdrawing the items, and found an odd sense of comfort in their malicious pasts. His older bones ached as he blinked through existence, finding the exact point where he knew he had to return to, mere moments after Cass had been killed.

Annabelle and Emily were being forced to the ground by the brute force of the officers, wiggling to free themselves. Atari watched helplessly as a body rose behind them, unbeknownst to any of the struggling figures. Cass's body rose to its feet as if pioneered by invisible wires, shambling aimlessly for a second as the lodged bullet was ripped from her inner mechanisms, dropping to the ground with a rattling thump. All four pairs of eyes turned in unison, spotting the reanimated corpse far too late as it tackled the one officer, tearing shreds off his jugular with rapacious teeth. The lanky man squealed, blood whipping onto the floor as his partner fumbled to reclaim his firearm. The clambering body of Cass left the man a twitching husk, clawing at a relentless spigot of gushing blood.

Atari watched the other officer fire blindly, taking potshots at the creature that inhabited her body as it pounced towards him. She grew in stature, limbs elongating with each stride, the features diminished as they stretched to fit their new frame until nothing defining Cass remained. It barreled into the man, making quick work of his limbs, ripping them outwards until the sinews that desperately clung to his joints severed, a sadistic whip in their snapping. He screamed. God, did he scream, as his limbs were ripped from his frame, taking stringy snaps of cheese-like skin that popped as bones crackled like a car running over a stick.

The man dropped, armless, to his knees, still screaming as the beast tossed his arms aside, prying his jaw open with its muscular fingers. It tore in one fluid movement, ripping the man's lower jaw from its joint and thrusting it clear across the room. The man gurgled on perforated bone fragments, his tongue lulling without a mouth to catch it as he quivered for an endless second before dropping to join the pile of corpses on the ground.

Atari's heart left him as he watched the creature gallop towards Emily, plucking her from the ground and raising her high in the air. Atari held his breath, preparing for his plan to fail, when the beast opened an orifice that had once been its mouth, pouring a blackened ooze from its stretched lips which rained directly into Emily's mouth, infecting her while draining the corpse until it began to revert to Cass's shape, both figures struggling against each other.

Atari took his shot, holding up the lighter that sprayed a thick, unreal flame, lapping up the air with its lustful tongue that erupted a small fireball from his palm. He dropped it, watching the floor erupt into flames upon contact, the gasoline they had sprayed it with earlier doing the trick. The fire spread rapidly, plunging forward where it struck the vile ooze which recoiled in agony. Even without a face to emote, Atari could tell it was pained by the seizure it collapsed into.

He watched as the creature split itself in two, one half continuing its onslaught down Emily's throat as the other half launched through the air towards him. The ooze crawled, as if its tendrils were a hand, grappling for Atari's throat, where it began to slither its way inside. Pain. The same searing, agonizing, endless pain as taking the pills. Atari closed his eyes, waiting what felt like forever for it to be over. His mind collapsed in on itself, vision shifting around total nothingness. He struggled to keep his hands from letting go of the rope and pistol.

When he felt as though he might explode, he came to in a Dante-esque world of disembodied limbs which withered and writhed, collecting the entirety of his view in their greedy grasp. His eyes pivoted, hand spinning with the Glock facing forward as Gal's corpse shambled back into view, a mirror image coming from every direction at once. They charged, squealing him down despite the mouth never moving, and Atari fired off a potshot, the pistol driving a slug directly through the creature's head. It paused in place. Just paused entirely for moments on end before erupting into a series of spasms, more a blade of grass in the wind than a human body.

The ooze began expanding out of the bullet hole, rising into the air where it levitated in great plumes, all combining until they formed the deranged framework of the beast from Atari's visions, coming in clearer than ever. Atari watched it, its details almost reflecting Emily's in that weird, off-kilter manner of a puddle. He watched it momentarily flicker with her eyes. A noose wrapped around its throat for a second.

Atari plunged the Glock into the nothingness, past the wiggling masses of limbs and began firing off shot after shot until he had emptied the chamber. Each gunshot passed through the beast, dragging its innards with it as they funneled out its back like tendrils, only stopping when they lost all momentum. The beast didn't move, nor did it react in any capacity.

Atari let the drugs take him further, their presence giving him more control over his environment as he pushed himself mentally back to reality, catching the chaos once more.

Emily rose, that glimmer of possession creeping over her eyes as her body jerked towards the center of the room, stepping directly on top of one of the officers as she made a beeline for the stairs. Atari followed, dragging along his length of rope as Emily procured her own, winding up the stairs as they raced each other, tying the rope along the rungs with diligent hands.

There was a single moment of hesitation as Atari questioned his plan, looking into the void that took up Emily's eyes. He clawed at the rope, affixing the noose at the same time as Emily, marketing folds with the same precision. His eyes kept bouncing between the device and Emily, as if testing his own resolve. Emily stood on a chair, delicately placing the noose around her neck, face still void of humanity as Atari did the same. Emily stepped into nothingness, and Atari paralleled the movement, delving into the spotlight iris of a great abyss. His body flooded with a mixture of fear and ecstatic exasperation. Simultaneously, they dropped, snapping backward with the force of the rope. They writhed, reaching for their necks with failing fingers.

Where Atari fought alone, a force rose from the floor, Annabelle joining Emily where she struggled to hoist her hanging friend within the air. He watched as she fought against the flailing limbs that pummeled her. Still, Annabelle continued to struggle, claws digging into Emily's throat. They were her eyes. Once again. Her eyes. Once again, she wore the same exact eyes she had every other moment of their existence in his world. Those beautiful, endless orbs sobbed now, fluids leaking in great geysers.

Atari hung there, his neck bones dislodging in his throat. He could feel his Adam's apple growing tighter, muscles constricting around it, desperate for oxygen. He saw the beast, once again standing in the corner of the room, taunting him as it lumbered in an unmoving stance. Saw it pure, as it should be viewed, in such a way that was impossible to describe or even remember for more than that split second of sight. Still, his eyes moved on from the Lovecraftian grandeur, focusing only on Emily as she was slowly lowered to the ground. His heart fluttered as Annabelle pumped Emily's chest, doing her best to perform CPR. He waited, baited fear in the last of his breath, until her chest began to rise.

21

27

PRESENT

ANNABELLE HOBBLED UP TO the cradle, her legs quivering a bit under the pressure of holding up her body. The bedside machines twittered and buzzed, projecting a claustrophobic web of robotic parts and wires that snaked under the man's skin, keeping him alive. Annabelle moved in just as mechanical fashion, almost as if an automaton wore her skin. She hunched her back, dropping into the framework of the chair as she lumbered over him, carefully caressing his arm with her long, pasty fingers.

She felt footsteps behind her, then the company of a hand pressed into her shoulder, causing her body to twitch. A warm breath ravished her ear, the tiny interior hairs standing as if in salute. Painstakingly, her head turned, eyeing Emily as she spoke through a nasally spell, interjected with a raspiness as if she had been duel wielding Newports for years. "You ready for this?"

Annabelle felt her head nod before she had even processed the phrase.

"You sure?"

Another nod. Annabelle studied Emily's face. Wide, puffy eyes sunken in on a coat of sleepy haze. A quivering lip that fought to hold back her lingering fear. The scars of brush burn straddling her neck, a grooved marking that haloed the noose's imprint onto her skin, even after these past few days.

"Then let's do this...together?" Emily held out a pinky, waiting for Annabelle to take hold.

"Together," Annabelle stated in her best attempt at a confident tone.

Annabelle opened her mouth to call out when the canvas wall around them stripped open, exposing them to the ICU hall. Stale air crept inside immediately. Brisk, with a smell like cleaner and supplements and the banshee-esque chorus of ringing cyborgs, each body adapted to the machinery supporting their individual life cycle. Quiet. It was densely quiet, almost as if sound had forgotten it was supposed to exist at all outside the bubble Emily and Annabelle had crafted for themselves.

Then the doctors entered the room, and brought with them sound, and life, and panic, and metal utensils of varying sizes and utilities. They brought color, somehow, in their white paper jumpsuits and aprons. Annabelle had to pull Emily a bit, tugging her out of the way as she remained rooted like a deer in their headlamps. They both edged the room, leaning back for the fear of their legs giving out, Annabelle's hand still unconsciously plucking at Emily's shirt, and only just then noticed that the shirt had been Atari's, the stretched text on the back a quote from one of his favorite bands.

Atari. Her mind flickered back to her dying friend heaving on the ground, foaming a viscous fluid that peppered his jaw in milky bubbles. She watched him die. She had been watching him die. Over and over. Each time she'd feel the coarse frays of the rope in her hands, peeling at its pincushion layers in a desperate attempt to separate them from Emily's neck and she'd be forced to turn her back on her best friend. To miss his final breath.

She gripped the cooled stone wall, dragging herself back to reality as she watched the doctors prepare for the removal, testing Trigger's lungs and throat with various devices she couldn't identify or accurately describe. In her head, she screamed at them, fending them off her friend like a wake of vultures, making damn sure the world couldn't hurt him any further. She knew the risks of a coma, this long, of a body this strained. Brain damage. PTSD. A lack of anything left to call human.

She held the wall as if restraining herself would stop her pouncing on one of the doctors, and instead watched as the tube was deliberately removed from his throat, each agonizing tug revealing more of a mushy, bile coated tubing like a magician's handkerchief, endless and aimless.

Annabelle could feel Emily shift her weight, scrunching up her toes. The last of the piping was plucked from his throat with a moist plop, whisked away by a hydra of doctors, replicating more to take their place. One of the doctors in the outer circle looked towards Emily and Annabelle, speaking through his procedural mask. "He's breathing!"

Relief. A sudden, overpowering sense of relief for the first time in what seemed like weeks. Annabelle could breathe. He was alive. He didn't wake. Not at first. Instead buried in a sense of half wake as his eyes would flutter senselessly open, no world behind them. Eyes that extended so far past a mortal frame that they might as well not exist entirely.

Then, out of nowhere, and for a single second, he spoke.

ABOUT THE AUTHOR

I'M JUST A WEIRDO who constantly measures mantras between 'in omnia paratus' and 'memento mori.' I love puzzlework poems and songs that require research to decipher the full meaning of turning poems into games of their own meaning. I am the author of CALL TO THE VOID DEFINITIVE EDITION and SLEEPING AMONG WOLVES. I am excited to share with you my longest and most personal piece yet.

I would like to extend a sincere thank you to anyone that has picked up this messy, uncomfortable fraction of my soul. With each person who reads my book that is helped along in their own journey by a handful of words, I have to say that my purpose is fulfilled a bit more. Remember to never stop fighting for yourself or your art, as we all struggle for our own sense of permanence. And again, thank you!